J.J. Hebert Endorsement

Eerie and thought-provoking, author James Johnson's novel An American Abduction is fiendishly difficult to put down. Once you think you've figured out where it's going, there's another surprise twist right around the corner. When you combine great characters and the supernatural with thrilling action, how can you go wrong? Don't be surprised if this killer story makes you start to think alien life truly exists.

AN
AMERICAN ABDUCTION

IS IT FICTION,
OR IS IT HAPPENING?

JAMES A JOHNSON

An American Abduction

Copyright © 2023 by James A Johnson. All rights reserved.

FOREWORD

We all have a natural fascination with the supernatural. On a cultural level, Hollywood movies and books in all genres repeatedly raise the question of if we're alone in the universe and what extraterrestrials might look like and do. There's an interest in what's out there that will never die out, and it shouldn't, because as beings who are alive, we are interested in life in all of its possible forms.

On a personal level, many of us have grown up with stories of UFO sightings or alien contact or there being aliens among us. In the same breath we're told that they're not real and that those things couldn't possibly happen, but we're always resistant to that, reserving a space for them deep in our hearts. We want to believe in them because the one thing we know for sure is that there is more present in this universe than we could possibly imagine.

An American Abduction captures this part of our imaginations through the eyes of a young couple, Matt and Tangie, who find themselves in extraordinary circumstances once they embrace the possibility that what they see with their eyes and know through our culture is not the be all and end all of existence. They use their smarts and their love for each other to realize that there is a whole world around us that we're not privy to with our blinders on and the news media ringing in our ears.

What James Johnson does is challenge us to get out of our own little boxes and to imagine what kind of possibilities really exist in the world. We're excited by the idea of secret government programs and foreign adversaries wielding semi-automatic rifles, but the real villain of this story is the metaphorical straight jacket they wear when they parrot the conventional wisdom that these things can't possibly exist.

Let's eject conventional wisdom. Cast aside what you've been told can't be. Stop denying the possibility that we're not alone or that we're not able to be affected in some way by things that are happening outside of this planet. There's phenomena that occurs every single day that can't be explained by the naked eye or by scientists. And the truth is we don't have to understand it. We just have to witness it and be open to the possibility. I've spent a significant amount of time in my life exploring the paranormal and the supernatural. There are places on this earth that anyone could go to and have a better than even chance of experiencing something that defies the expectations we generally set for our everyday lives. But most people won't ever seek out these places, and they won't pick up books like this one that challenge them to think about the world in a bigger way.

Do you know why? They're still trapped in the box.

By picking up *An American Abduction*, you've already kicked a hole through one of the boards. You can see the light shining through. Another kick with your heel will make the hole bigger. Another few pages in, and you'll start to see something that makes you wonder. Keep kicking, keep reading, and keep fighting against these stale norms we live by, and you'll make a big enough hole for you to get out of the box. Come join us. We're free. Anything is possible.

—Mariel Hemingway,
Oscar-nominated actress and author,
granddaughter of Nobel Prize-winning
novelist Ernest Hemingway

THANKS AND ACKNOWLEDGMENT

First, I want to thank my Lord and Savior Jesus Christ. It was God who sent me the idea for this book in a dream. I thought my book-writing days were over. But God had other plans. That tells me there are certain truths He wanted me to bring out in the book.

Even though I believed the idea and plan for this book came from God, I sat on the thought of the book for two years before I wrote anything. I had a hard time finding the motivation and ideas. I don't think this is that unusual, even when God directs our paths. God doesn't always give us the big picture, probably because it would be too much to comprehend. We have to step out on faith.

When I did start writing, I wrote a couple chapters, then put the book away for several more months, nearly another year.

That's where my wife came in, who I want to thank for providing the initial motivation I needed to get this project going in earnest. When she read the manuscript, she thought the book was funny, but also felt she learned a lot from it.

That told me the book will mean different things to different people. That keeps me from categorizing the book. It may fit okay in the religious, fiction, or maybe even nonfiction sections of the bookstore.

I also want to thank my church. My pastors teach about God's love, and that He wants us to be successful. One of my pastors taught a sermon on the potential we have in us. One of the things he specifically said is that there may be a book in us waiting to come out.

I also want to thank all of my family, friends, and others who supported and motivated me. They inspired and encouraged me to keep writing. Many of them helped by critiquing this book.

Special thanks to Mike Campbell, my longtime friend, who encouraged me, and provided good knowledge and advice.

Special thanks to my brother-in-law Mark Scheidweiler, who read my manuscript, and provided critical analysis of the book.

Special thanks to my friend Aaron Hargrove, who also provided critical analysis of the book.

And a very special thanks to the Blocker family, Ty and Ariel. You showed much faith in me, and provided so much encouragement, and convinced me that writing was my calling from God.

And a special shout-out to those family members who are also writers, like my brother David, who is in the process of writing his own book. Other relatives have also written books. This provided the final motivation I needed to finish this book. They reminded me that literary talent runs in the family.

No book is a one-person project. It is a collaborative effort. And I thank God for sending those people to help me. God works through people to get His work done.

CONTENTS

CHAPTER

1

FIRST ABDUCTION

A man in his camper drove deep into a forest in southwestern New Mexico. His son sat in the front seat with him eating some potato chips and looking at the wooded scenery.

"Pretty nice view of the trees, isn't it?" he questioned his son.

"Yes, Dad," his son answered. "I've been looking forward to this trip for some time. Do you think we will see some rattlesnakes?"

"I hope not," his father answered. "But I hope we see some other nicer wildlife."

"We're almost where I want to park and set up our camper for the night. We will be close to a stream where we will fish for our dinner. Hopefully we will catch some trout and have a nice outdoor dinner. We will make a fire and fry the fish by the campfire."

Later that evening, the two campers sat by the campfire eating the fish they had caught.

"Nothing like catching and frying fresh fish on the campfire." the father stated.

"Yes, Dad," his son stated while eating his fish.

"This camping trip is long overdue," his father said.

"If your mother had not been taken from us by that drunk driver, she would be here with us."

"Yeah. I miss Mom." "Me too."

"I'm glad I finally decided to change jobs, which provides more free time for us."

"Yeah, Dad."

"You never told me much about your other job."

"Well, I'll just leave it in the past, and we'll move on. That job was not what I needed. This is a whole new life for us."

"We got rid of that house. We can stay in hotels and this small camper until we find a new home."

A round bright orb moved across the night sky headed toward the campers.

"I wonder what that moving white light is up there in the sky," the son said, as he pointed toward the night sky.

"I don't know," his father answered.

"But you know there are lot of moving objects in the sky, even in the sparsely populated areas of New Mexico."

"Think about meteors, meteorites, comets. Not to mention all of the man-made stuff. You know New Mexico is where the first atomic bomb was tested and exploded."

"Yes, I know," his son responded.

"But that thing looks like it sees us, and is coming toward us." They both stared up at the object as it approached.

"That's no meteor," the father said. The object approached and started slowing down as it focused on the two people.

"I'm getting scared, Dad!" his son said in a loud tone, grabbing his father.

"I'm really scared!" his son yelled, and the object stopped and hovered over them.

The object shot a beam of light down on the father.

"Run, son!" the father commanded, as the beam of light held him immovable.

His son ran away fast through the woods. The beam levitated his father up into the orb. His son ran until he found a large dead tree to hide under.

He could look through a crack in the log, and saw the light moving through the woods. He felt the spacecraft was looking for him.

He was shaking as the light came closer. He tried to be quiet, but he was breathing very fast because he had run hard to the log, and was extremely scared.

The beam of light came closer and closer. The light came to about five feet from him before it stopped.

The light quickly moved back to the camper the father and son had taken for the camping trip.

The light found the camper. Then, a ray of light shot through the beam to the camper.

The camper exploded into bits and pieces. The explosion shook the boy.

The beam retracted to the round orb. Then the craft shot up and disappeared into the night sky.

The boy peeked out into the sky. He slowly exited from under the log, and then continued running through the woods.

2

ANOTHER ABDUCTION

F our men sat at a table in a high-rise office building in downtown Albuquerque, New Mexico.

"Look," the first man stood up and addressed the other three. "I know you all are losing patience with the process, but these kinds of things take time."

"Bill," one of the men addressed him, "you are the supervisor of operations of Level Four, and the president of America First. Surely you can get things going faster. Our company is waiting. How much longer should we keep such technology under wraps? We stand to make billions, and change the world."

"Charlie," Bill answered. "These things take time, and I only want to change America. We are working with the CIA, the military, the US Patent Office, and private partners, all in secrecy, trying to get this work done. It's a delicate balancing act."

"The CIA wants to keep these projects hush hush. They have to find a way to get the President of the United States on board with the products, or get him out of the way so he can't keep you from utilizing these products."

"And the kicker is that we all want to keep these technologies in American hands as long as we can. I don't have the easiest job right now." "I would think our military, and even our Central Intelligence Agency, would want to use these devices as soon as possible." The third man at the table spoke up. "Anything that makes our armed forces stronger should be

fast tracked, not slowed down."

"Gentlemen," Bill addressed, "the military leaders who do know about those secret projects are anxious to do field tests, and I can understand that. But the CIA wants to be a little more careful. We are talking about things that will change the world as we know it."

"I think the CIA wants control of everything," the fourth man in the room spoke up. "I don't think they want to share the power with the military. And I know they don't want the NSA to know anything. The President is using the NSA to get information about the facility. And the CIA fears the President will go public with the information, or want the projects stopped."

"I think you're right." Bill agreed. "I'm trying to manage an ego contest between powerful people over very powerful toys, while also keeping other powerful people out of the loop."

"The work we do is top secret. I know you all are looking at the finish line. But this is a long slow race that will be well worth it when we get there." "The CIA and military leaders have put full trust and confidence in

me to get things done in the way they need to be done. We are talking about things not even Area Fifty-One knows about. There are even things that I can't discuss with you guys. Not to mention how I have to handle staff to keep them in the dark and honest about operations and goals."

"Yes, Bill," the third man answered. "You hold a lot of power, and you are as clandestine as you need to be. I personally borrowed a lot of money to get into this because I fully expect a return a thousand-fold. I can't do anything at this point but be patient. Just keep us posted."

"I will let you know what I can let you know when I know it." Bill responded.

"We should conclude this meeting. I'll talk to you all again next month. Good day, gentlemen."

The three men shook Bill's hand and left the office. Bill picked up his phone and dialed a number.

"Hello." he said to the person who answered the phone on the other end. "Things are on schedule. America First will be the most powerful organization in the world."

Bill turned off his phone, closed his briefcase, and left the room.

He entered the elevator and pushed the parking lot button. The elevator lowered him to the parking lot level. He exited the elevator, started walking to his car, and pulled his car keys from his pocket. Then he pulled out a pack of cigarettes and started to pull his cigarette lighter from his pocket.

A black Chevrolet SUV pulled up and stopped where Bill stood at his car. Two men jumped out with guns.

"Bill Moyer?" one of the men called.

"Who are you?" Bill responded, with his hands in the air. "Just come with us!" the second man ordered.

They cuffed his hands, put a hood over his head, and pushed him into the vehicle. The vehicle sped off.

"Mister Moyer." the man who sat in the front passenger seat declared as he turned around.

"Who wants to know?" Bill asked again.

"Many people want to know you, Mr. Moyer." the man answered.

Many powerful people."

"You have a track record of abductions and reverse engineering work. Well, just consider yourself now abducted and about to be reverse engineered."

3

A MATCH MADE IN HEAVEN

"You may now kiss the bride," the minister said, and Matt Riley and his bride Tangie Turner turned to each other, smiled, and engaged in a three-second lip massage. They then turned and walked briskly down the aisle to thundering applause from family, friends, and other attendees in the large nondenominational church in down- town Boston. Included in that crowd were Matt's proud father Luke, and Tangie's parents. Matt's mother, Abigail died of breast cancer when he was five years old.

They walked down the church stairs where they were greeted by a chauffeur opening the door for them to enter a stretch Mercedes limousine. The crowd followed and offered a barrage of hugs and kisses.

A half hour later, they arrived at the convention center for the wedding reception. They entered to another roaring applause. The band they hired for the reception started playing. It was a soul band, with a beautiful female lead singer. The band started and played top soul songs from the 1970's and 1980's as requested from both families. Everyone danced after the groom and bride started dancing.

Luke danced with one of the maids of honor up to Matt. "Son, you got yourself a good little woman, and you're headed for a great life," he said.

"I know. I'm a lucky man," Matt answered, and Tangie smiled. "May I dance with your beautiful bride?" the best man at the wedding asked Matt, as the music played.

"Sure." Matt answered to the African American man with a big smile. "It's the least I can do for you, Julius. You have done so much for me here in Boston. We have had a lot of good times. You've been my best friend." "Now you got a new best friend," Julius answered. "A good one for life." "You can't get rid of me that easily, Julius," Matt responded. "You're a friend for life as well. You're smarter than I am. You're going to find a good woman too. And you're going to be very successful."

Three hours later, the couple left the convention center to hugs and well wishes, and entered the limousine for a trip to Logan Airport. They were going on a two-week honeymoon tour of Germany. They wanted to see old German castles, and the places where Adolf Hitler once reigned.

Tangie's parents were full of tears throughout most of the wedding and reception. They were delighted that their daughter had met and married into wealth. They were also very happy she graduated into what they believed would be a very well-paying job in her field. They struggled through average jobs to raise her and put her through school. She would not have been able to attend college without the aid of the scholarship she earned for being an honor student.

Matt grew up privileged, but had not traveled a lot. He was more of a book nerd, but he loved sports. Luke was dedicated to his work, even more so after he lost his wife. Tangie grew up wanting to travel. She was a history buff, and Germany was one of those places that fascinated her. She dreamed of the day that she could see and walk the very grounds where Adolf Hitler had reigned, although she viewed him as an evil antichrist.

The two Yale biomedical engineering honor graduates met in an undergraduate class. Although they grew up in different parts of the United States, Matt in New Jersey and Tangie in Texas, they seemed to be of one heartbeat and destined to spend their adult lives together.

Matt received his Bachelor's Degree in Biophysics and Structural Biology. Tangie earned her undergraduate degree in Molecular Cell Biology. Both earned their Master's Degrees in Biomedical Sciences. Neither one wanted to be a doctor or work in health care. Instead, they wanted to do research in human biometrics, brain functions, artificial intelligence, and develop cures for diseases and mental dysfunctions.

Matt was a handsome kid, and grew up being adored by all the girls in school and the neighborhood. And he became a prime target for the coeds on the campus of Yale University, a private institution in New Haven, Connecticut.

Tangie had won her share of beauty contests since she was a baby. This included cutest baby contests, junior miss contests, and prom queen in high school. Early in life, her parents groomed her to use her looks to pave the way for making a better life for herself than the struggle and sacrifice they had raising her. They were confident that their pretty blonde child was a gift from God, and would have a much better life than they ever had. Ironically, Matt was born in Houston, Texas. But his father moved them to New Jersey after his mother died. Luke desired to be something of a Texas oil Wall Street wiz, and fulfilled that desire after he lost his wife, who was a diehard Texan.

Luke made his fortune in the oil industry when living and working in Houston, Texas. After he made enough of a fortune as an oil broker in Texas, he moved to New Jersey because he wanted to be closer to New York City, the financial capital of America.

He wanted to mingle with the power brokers of the world, but not actually live in New York. So, he built a palatial estate in the East Orange, New Jersey suburbs. And he planned for his only son to receive a college education from one of the top scholastic institutions in the world.

Although growing up in New Jersey, the twenty-five-year-old Yale Summa Cum Laude student had Texas blood. He dreamed of living in the western or southwestern parts of the United States. He grew up watching the old west programs such as Gunsmoke, Bonanza, and The Big Valley on the cable channels that played those old western shows. His dad grew up watching westerns, and passed this fascination on to his son.

His dad was an avid hunter and gun collector. He had a room dedicated with all kind of guns, from pistols, to shotguns, automatic weapons, including AK 47s, and automatic pistols. He taught Matt how to shoot all of those weapons. Matt applied his math and science intellect to the art of firing a weapon at a target.

Growing up through his teen years, Matt collected Native American arrowheads, artifacts, and toy western style guns. And of course, he loved wearing cowboy boots, and playing cowboys and Indians with his child-hood friends and family whenever he was with them.

Matt also loved sports, although the only sport he played was golf. He played on his high school golf team. Luke loved golf, and was a member of many private golf clubs. Luke learned to love golf because most wealthy people he knew at work and in the upper-class neighborhoods he lived in were golfers.

Like most amateur golfers, Matt struggled with the game. Most of the world's amateur golfers don't break ninety on a regular basis, and Matt was firmly entrenched in that majority. He took golf lessons, and practiced his game regularly, but never raised his level of proficiency to meet his goals. He felt he should be shooting no higher than the low eighties on a bad day. His dream was to be a scratch golfer, shooting in the mid and lower seventies on a regular basis. The one frustration in his life was that he felt golf courses were beating him. He didn't think so much of beating the competitors he played with, but putting the ornery golf course in its proper place. As a result of not meeting his golfing goal, he left more rounds of golf frustrated than satisfied. This made him often entertain the thought of giving up golf. This periodic thought was therapeutic. It made him realize that he had control over the golf demons by just getting rid of his golf clubs. The rationale was that he would have peace of mind by just not participating. But like most golfers, he could not stop going back to the place that caused him so much pain.

Tangie knew of Matt's golf addiction. She chose not to share this part of his life with him, but rather let them use his time on the links as "me" time for both of them. This routine started in college, and she felt it would be a healthy benefit to their marriage.

Matt never cared for life on the east coast. He got a lot of joy looking at the pictures of his father growing up in Texas, complete with the cow- boy hats and spur boots. He also had family back in Texas who would rib him about growing up an easterner, and would tell him that he was not a true Texan.

He longed to live somewhere in the southwest or western part of the country. He wanted the openness, mountains, canyons and topography that made up the western United States. He didn't care for the congested traffic and rudeness of the people of the eastern seaboard.

He also didn't care for living in the eastern time zone. When he would talk to his friends and relatives in Texas and further west, and they would mention the time, he felt he was losing time by being an hour to three hours ahead of those time zones.

Tangie was born and raised in Saginaw, Texas, an inner suburb of Fort Worth. Although she was a beauty queen, her parents didn't allow her to spend much time with boys. They did not want her to be distracted from her schoolwork and her religious roots. They raised her in a fairly strict traditional Baptist church and lived by many of the outdated Old Testament laws of living.

They also wanted her to be a strong and independent person financially, emotionally, and physically so she would not have to depend on anyone. She learned five self-defense disciplines; Karate, Boxing, Mauy Thai, Jiu-Jitsu, and Krav Maga.

They were not a bit concerned that their daughter married a man not sold on Christianity. They looked at it as an opportunity for their deeply religiously reared child to convert him from someone headed for hell to a saved Christian who would help her convert others. This would fulfill Jesus' command to go out and spread the gospel of Christianity to all of the world.

Most attendees to Tangie's church, including her parents, dressed formally for Sunday service. She could not wear her sneakers to church. Her parents believed dancing was a sin. The men who wore hats promptly removed their lids when they entered the sanctuary. Her mother never wore pants. Chewing gum in church was a no no. She believed God was sitting there waiting for her to sin and then punish her in some way for that sin. She thought eating pork, as one of Moses' laws to the Israelites of the Old Testament, was a sin.

Further, she was told that speaking in tongues, as the great Saint Paul elaborated on in the first book of Corinthians, was to be ignored. Her pas- tor did not teach that Christians had, or should have, the power to heal and be healed from any affliction, in accord with Jesus's teachings. She believed God had a date for people to die, and they could not do anything about changing the day God planned for people to die. Her religious upbringing did not make much of a differentiation of the Old Testament from the New Testament.

Some of Tangie's young girl-friends in junior high and high school who had migrated from denominational to nondenominational churches would compare their teachings to her teachings and beliefs. Her non-denominational girlfriends impressed her about their church teachings. They would say things such as they wore their everyday clothes to church. They were taught that the Old Testament laws were replaced by the new covenant of the New Testament, which govern people today. They explained that their pastors taught the entire Bible, not ignoring any parts or scriptures. They learned that God is a God of love, not punishment. They learned that people blamed the devil's evil deeds on God.

Most importantly, Tangie's friends taught her that accepting Jesus as her Lord and Savior was the one and only way to get to heaven. All of that religious dressing and traditional stuff of her church did nothing to get her closer to her heavenly home.

She promptly joined a nondenominational church in Boston when she left home and started school at Yale. She was able to sway her parents around to more new covenant thinking. She was also a Summa Cum Laude honor student.

4

OPPOSITES ATTRACT

lthough the newlyweds were a match made in heaven, they had some differences. However, those differences would not cause any problems in the marriage. Rather, as the saying goes; opposites attract, their differences became teaching moments to each other.

Tangie was a staunch God-fearing, church-going, Bible-reading, Jesus-loving Christian. Matt was more of an agnostic. He agreed to a church wedding because that was what Tangie wanted.

The few times the existence of God would come up in his life, it was hard for him to conceive that a being had been here forever, and started life on earth. The Theory of Evolution made a little more sense to him.

Matt's father stopped going to church when his wife died. Luke was not raised in church. He only attended when he started dating Matt's mother. He attended because that was a way of getting on the good side with her. However, he was not a believer. And when Abigail died, Luke lost all interest in going to church, questioning why God would take such a great wife and mom when he and Matt needed her.

Not much church was discussed at home when Abigail was alive because Luke only showed superficial interest. She did not drill Bible reading and praying into Matt because she didn't want to upset Luke. She also believed if she pushed him too hard, he would resist even more, and feared Luke would take his side. This left Matt using his own young mind to try to determine if God was real.

His friends left him more confused because some were believers in Jesus while others were not. Being more of a concrete thinker, he had a hard time trying to accept the concept that one being saw and knew what every person on earth was doing at the same time, and knew what everyone was thinking.

One minor difference between the two was that Tangie loved animals, having grown up with a pet dog. Matt did not care for animals, at least not as pets. This was another trait he inherited from his father. Luke felt dealing with a pet just took time from being productive in other areas of life such as work and raising children.

This would be an insignificant difference in that the couple agreed they may not have any pets, although Tangie loved dogs. When they would discuss married life prior to their nuptials, Matt had mentioned that they may have no time for pets, with promising and demanding careers ahead of them. Having children would be another aspect of their marriage they agreed they would discuss after their careers were firmly established. They both wanted to have children at some point.

One big difference between the two was about extraterrestrial life. Tangie was a strong believer that life existed in places other than planet Earth, and that the planet was being inhabited by those visitors.

One night as a child she saw an object in the sky hovering over her house. She stared at the red blinking orb for about ten seconds when it dropped down into position and drew her attention up from playing with her dog. Then, in the blink of an eye, the oval-shaped light shot across the sky, leaving her staring up several minutes wondering what had she just seen.

She was already a believer in UFOs before this incident. She loved watching movies, TV programs, and cartoons that featured visitors from another planet who did not look like Earth dwellers. That night she saw the UFO cemented her belief in alien beings. She even preferred outer space and space alien toys over girly toys like dolls, playhouses, and hair articles.

She preferred reading books on outer space, aliens, and space travel rather than other types of books and magazines.

Since Matt struggled to believe in a living God, he certainly dismissed the idea of alien beings from other worlds. He couldn't comprehend life or entities anywhere except on Earth. He didn't accept that beings looked anything resembling the forms portrayed in the movies or the alien toys and pictures he saw everywhere.

He viewed children who believed in UFOs as people with strong imaginations. He would get into arguments, and even almost fought with those kids who believed UFOs were real.

As he grew older, he felt grownups who believed in UFOs were people with psychiatric issues who needed professional help to come back to the real world. He categorized those individuals as the ones who could not come up with creative ideas that would help in real world situations.

He felt that he was the exact opposite. He looked at himself as one who could create and develop solid answers and cures for the problems facing mankind.

Naturally, whenever the subject of UFOs came up, Matt and Tangie would strongly defend their beliefs, trying to apply logic they hoped the other would understand.

Tangie's logic to Matt was along the lines of trying to make him look beyond small-minded thinking that Earth was the only place within billions and billions of bodies in endless space where life existed.

Matt's retort was simply that no believer had produce an authentic item that he can look at, touch, or communicate with to prove it was from another world. He reasoned that everybody can imagine and anybody can make up stories for a variety of reasons. He believed some people imagined things unworldly to escape reality, fight boredom, entertain children, outdo competing storytellers, or have a mental illness. He further concluded that being imaginative of the unreal had been an asset that has profited people and companies, especially movie makers and book writers. However, he loved Tangie and didn't apply much of his assessment to her. He felt she was mainly using her view as a kind of way of keeping them from being too much alike, and would just make for healthy arguments. Since both knew well about each other's background by the time they married, and both were skilled learners, they welcomed the opportunity for each to state their case for the things they believed. They looked at it as a challenge to their persuasive abilities, and as an opportunity to make the other an even better person.

Matt and Tangie carried the kind of scholastic achievements that garnered attention from every corner of the world. All throughout their college careers, they were pursued by hundreds of organizations looking to bring them on board.

They were offered high-six-figure incomes from chemical engineering companies, hospitals, medical research facilities, military branches, regional and foreign governments, and millionaire entrepreneurs. Russia and China recruited them to work for them.

Johns Hopkins offered them high positions as biochemists or biophysicists at their research facilities. The Centers for Disease Control also wanted the couple to come to work for them.

Since most of the organizations knew the couple were dating in college, and later engaged, they would offer to hire both of them. The two often went on joint interviews, or the organization would offer to hire the other one without interviewing the other.

Both of them knew they wanted to live somewhere in the southwestern United States. Tangie told Matt that she wanted to move back to Texas, or live in New Mexico. She thought it would be neat to live in or near Roswell. It was near Roswell, where an alleged UFO crashed in 1947.

This story had always fascinated her. She thought it would be so neat to tell people she lived near the site of the crash. She also wanted to be able to visit the site on a regular basis, as her own homage to the local UFO legend.

They also wanted to be close to their family and friends. Luke planned to retire back to Texas.

CHAPTER

5

THE JOB OFFER

L uckily for the perfect couple beginning the perfect life, right before their graduations, an unknown government agency sought out the two looking to hire them on the spot.

The super-secret agency was given the name Global Observation Defense, or G.O.D. The name was chosen partly because if the employees were ever interrogated, they could say they work for God, and pass polygraph tests without giving away the secret agency.

The jobs at GOD appealed to the couple right off the bat, because when they were approached on campus by a stranger in a black suit, the cloak and dagger scenario fascinated them.

Six months before the couple married, the two took a break from classes and had lunch at a restaurant not far from campus. A middle-aged man approached the couple at their table. They were the only people at the table. The man, dressed in all black, including a black turtleneck sweater, walked up to them, bent over as if wanting to whisper a secret to the couple, and spoke their names. He looked each of them straight into their eyes as he called out their names.

"Mr. Matthew Lucas Riley, Ms. Tangie Abigale Turner?" the stranger asked with certainty.

"Yes, yes," the couple answered respectively, with some unease, anxiety, and curiosity.

"May I have a seat?" he asked, as he pointed to the two unoccupied chairs at the table.

"Certainly" Matt answered, as he pointed to the chair next to him, and slid his chair slightly away from the open seat and toward Tangie.

"Nice day, and nice restaurant." the stranger commented as he took his seat.

"Yes, it is." both responded.

"My name is unimportant, but I know quite a bit about you two. Don't ask how, and besides, many of your accomplishments are public knowledge."

"I know about your honors and awards from Yale. Both of you have IQs that would measure well above Einstein's."

"Both of you graduated from high school early. I know about your awards and accomplishments since you both were very young. I know about all the beauty pageants, spelling bees, and academic competitions you have won, Ms. Turner. And I know you have five-degree black belts and other trophies in five martial arts disciplines."

"I know you are an expert marksman, Mr. Riley, winning skeet shooting, trap shooting, bullseye shooting, and pistol shooting events. Your father taught you to be ten times better than he ever was."

"You both speak at least five languages. You two can fix a Rubik's Cube, complete ten complex crossword puzzles, and finish other brain teasers before I could eat a sandwich."

"Both of you would have Intelligence Quotient scores in the two hundreds, but I know both of you believe IQ tests are fundamentally flawed because you are smart enough to see that the tests cannot fully account for the complex nature of the brain and human intellect. They cannot adequately test and measure emotions, attitudes, motivations, et cetera, and cannot adequately measure or predict a person's success or achievements in life. You two could probably come as close to developing an IQ test more comprehensive than anything out there."

"My agency has been in contact with Yale's honors programs and academic advisors the past couple years, and we are very interested in bringing you on board with our agency in research and development."

(This was only a partial true statement, as the secret agency used the FBI and other secret means to zero in on potential candidates for their program.)

Thinking the next step was to ask the stranger what agency he represented and what the jobs entailed, the two just looked at him with the certainty that he was going to continue with his presentation and answer the questions they had in mind, which he did.

"I know you two have been offered jobs from Fortune five hundred companies, major research centers, international government agencies, the United Nations, hospitals like Johns Hopkins, and so on. We want both of you to come on board with our top-secret government-related agency that works closely with the CIA."

"We advance artificial intelligence with humans. We research human and animal diseases, deformities, mental illnesses, germs, bacteria, epidemics, pandemics, and develop models, medicines, machines, prototypes, platforms and all types of cures for those world problems."

He continued, "We research and develop chemical and biological weaponry. We research and develop atmospheric, weather, geographic, and planetary causes, measurements, and responses."

Knowing he had covered all of the career opportunities the two were interested in, the agent then paused to allow them to absorb his information. He had an air of confidence about his presentation as he looked at the gleam in their eyes.

They were speechless for the moment, using the pause to allow their body language and eye movements to show the flattery and sense or power they were feeling about the opportunity.

The agent then added his closing argument for their services. "We have a laboratory and R&D center near Carlsbad, New Mexico, where you will be stationed. It works in conjunction with many organizations, including Los Alamos, the University of New Mexico, New Mexico State, the Department of Defense, the FBI, and of course the Central Intelligence Agency."

With those words, Matt's eyes grew brighter, and a slight smile came to his face, which he quickly tried to hide. But that was the selling point for him. He knew he badly wanted to live in that part of the country, and now a job in the Southwest was providing him his longtime dream.

Feeling he had reeled in the two scholars, the agent pulled out a sheet of paper.

"Here's our offer," he quipped, as he confidently slid a piece of paper across the table toward the couple.

"I believe you will find the offer very generous. These are unique jobs that only you will be working for us."

"Contact me when you're ready to talk," he said, as he stood up and tipped his hat.

"Good day," he said, and he quickly disappeared into the crowd. They looked down at the paper, which had both of their full names.

Each name had a seven-figure income bolded out beside their names. The numbers were more than twice what they had been offered by such prestigious places as John's Hopkins, The Mayo Clinic, the Department of Defense, the National Football League, over half of the Fortune 500 companies, and many overseas countries and organizations.

They looked at each other simultaneously with puzzled looks in their eyes.

"What kind of jobs are these?" Tangie asked. "What do we do now?"
"Find a house in New Mexico! Sounds like the dream jobs for us."

Matt answered, putting a period on the job searching process.

CHAPTER

6

RELOCATION

Where do you want me to put this lamp?" one of the movers asked as they finished unloading the large moving van to the Riley's new home in one of the wealthiest suburbs of Carlsbad, New Mexico.

"Over there." Tangie pointed and commanded as she and Matt held hands and looked around the spacious living room with big smiles on their faces. The movers put the last pieces of furniture in place in a four-bedroom house in the northeast part of the city.

"I can't believe how much house we got for the money." Tangie exclaimed as she gave Matt a happy smack on the lips.

"Well, we're lucky that the median house price in New Mexico is lower than the average home in America, even lower than the average home of this size in the state of New Mexico," Matt answered as he returned Tangie's kiss.

Knowing they would have children at some point, the couple decided to buy a large home and bypass the necessity of buying another home later. Since they knew they were in the best school district, and that they would be heavily involved in their work, they were making a move to minimize future distractions from their jobs.

The house was of modern architecture, combined with the typical pueblo adobe style prevalent in the Southwest, and particularly prevalent in New Mexico.

The first known people in New Mexico were Puebloans and Anasazi, who built homes of sun-dried clay bricks mixed with grass, and covered with a protective layer of mud. The Riley home only had a Puebloan resembling roof of layered clay shingles.

They stood in their front door and waved goodbye to the movers, as their bright new black Mercedes convertible coupe sat in the driveway.

"What do we do now, Mr. Riley?" Tangie asked. Matt hugged her and answered.

"Go get something to eat, Mrs. Riley. We have a nice kitchen, but neither one of us care much for cooking. And these rock yards in this part of the country means there is not much yard work to do."

Tangie leaned back, smiled, looked Matt in his eyes, and spoke.

"We get wonderfully paying jobs working together. We get a huge advance that allows us to buy a house back in the part of the country you wanted to move to. This is a dream come true. You didn't get your home state of Texas, but you are close enough. New Mexico is the next best thing. And Carlsbad is such a nice city, with water in a very dry state."

"Yes," Matt agreed.

"Life couldn't be better. I'm very close to Texas. You get to live near the place where you believe a UFO crashed, which will continue to feed your wild UFO beliefs," he said, as he twirled his finger in the air.

She smiled and responded.

"Yes, I believe there is life other than ours here on earth, and that we are being visited by those other beings."

He cut in.

"You also believe in a God you have never seen, and you also believe that you can convince me to believe in such things as aliens among us that can obliterate us any time they want to. You believe your God created this universe and built man in His own image. You believe nothing about the sensible evolution of man. I see we have a nice healthy set of issues to debate for the rest of our lives. A good debate that will only help us as curious and open-minded people."

"Yes, I believe in a God I haven't seen." she said.

"It's all about having faith. And I plan to join a church soon. One of a nondenominational nature, because I don't want to go where they are concerned about how they dress, and have such traditions and methodologies that are either Old Testament laws that we don't live under anymore, or are not even mentioned in the Bible at all. And I agree that we will have fun trying to convince each other of our beliefs or disbeliefs. I believe I will win the arguments."

"How can you win?" He questioned in a serious tone.

"You would have to show me your God, and I don't believe that is going to happen. You can't convince me by quoting Bible scriptures, and I doubt I will see you walk on water. I know that is in your Bible."

"And how are you going to convince me of non-worldly life? I can't be persuaded by looking up at some bright lights in the sky that I can't identify."

"And how do you explain that if God made man, then who made the aliens?"

"Well," she quipped. "I'm just concerned that you believe in God, and accept Jesus as your Lord and Savior. God doesn't want anyone to be lost to eternal damnation. I believe I can help change you because I have faith that it will happen, just like I have faith in God."

"Do you think we just got this opportunity on looks or luck? I firmly believe God put us where He wanted us to be. And I believe you will change your mind because you are open to the possibility. If you had a closed mind and were totally unholy, we might not be together because the Bible says not to be unequally yoked with people who turn you away from God."

"And as a Christian, it's my mission to help lead people to Jesus so they will be saved."

"And I don't know where aliens came from. I don't know if anyone knows where they come from. I just believe they exist. Not only are there billions of stars and celestial bodies, there are billions of galaxies that contain billions of celestial bodies including stars, planets, black holes, and other cosmic bodies."

"A lot of those galaxies are so far away it would take us millions of years to reach them, assuming we could provide an energy source that would last us long enough to get there. You would need robots to operate the spacecraft because no humans would live long enough for the trip. Space is endless, with endless possibilities. I think it's very closed-minded to think our Earth is the only place where life exists."

"I do believe one day I will know where aliens come from. God reveals to us the things we need to know."

She looked into Matt's eyes.

"You have a big heart, like me. We look to donate to several causes, including fighting breast cancer, which took your mother from you when you were only five years old."

"We want to volunteer our spare time and money helping less fortunate families, including inner-city communities. That tells me you have the loving foundation that will move you toward being a good Christian. And I want you to teach me golf. That shows I have an open mind."

Her mind suddenly went to their jobs.

"I'm so curious and excited about our jobs. We know nothing about what they want us to do. We don't know who we will be working with. We don't know our supervisors. We don't even know the mission of the organization. I hope we didn't just jump on the jobs because they pay really well, and also brought us to a part of America where you wanted to live." "We did want to live in this part of the country. I couldn't wait to get

out of that eastern time zone and those cold winters and rude people. But it was the mystery and unknown about the jobs that intrigued us about the opportunity. And if it doesn't work out, we can always go to any of the many employers who wanted to hire us in the first place."

They embraced with another kiss in their doorway when Matt's cell phone began ringing. "I wonder who this is," he said as he looked down at his phone. The caller ID showed 'No Caller.'

"Hello," he answered. Then a cryptic, computer-generated voice came on.

"Drive to Carlsbad Caverns in the morning at seven AM. You will receive more information as you arrive at the park." Then the phone clicked off.

Matt had a puzzled look on his face, then spoke.

"A computer voice said for us to drive to Carlsbad Caverns tomorrow morning at seven, and we will be given further instructions when we get there." he responded to Tangie's equally puzzled look, then he continued.

"Things are certainly intriguing and exciting. This is the most uncertainty we have ever experienced, but I fully believe we can handle it with flying colors. Let's get something to eat. What do you feel like eating?"

"Why don't we find a restaurant that has good southwestern food? You're back in the southwest. We might as well start with the food that this part of the country is known for."

"You're on!" he responded, as he reached to close the front door of the house. "But we won't know if it's good until we try it. But that's another thing I love about our new lives. We'll be trying new restaurants, stores, making new friends, and for you, new churches. That's almost as exciting as our new jobs."

"And let's put on some good old seventies music when we get back home. That's another thing my dad got me hooked on."

They hopped into their car and sped away.

A half hour later, the waiter led the couple to a table at a southwestern grill in downtown Carlsbad.

"I'm hungry, and I want to try several things," Matt declared as they sat down.

"I want burritos, chili, cactus fries, the works." he said as the waitress handed the two their menus.

"Next time we will try a great southwestern steak restaurant, but to- night it's totally southwestern fare."

After they placed their orders, Tangie reached over and grabbed Matt's hands.

"You know, this is so wonderful," she said, as they looked out the restaurant window.

"Most people don't realize it, but there's so many places to visit in New Mexico. I've done my research." She then started citing a litany of New Mexico's attractions.

"There's Carlsbad Caverns National Park, where we are going, with over one hundred known caves. There's White Sands National Monument, with pretty gleaming gypsum sand and sand dunes."

"Albuquerque has an international air balloon fiesta every autumn that we need to see. Old Town Albuquerque is in the downtown area. It's a bit of a tourist area, but you can see old-style buildings and meet the Native Americans who are selling the handicrafts they make."

"An old girlfriend of mine visited there and told me there's an old Mexican restaurant in the old town square that has a large very old tree still alive and growing right through the roof of one of the seating areas. She also said the restaurant serves the best pina coladas in the world."

"There's Roswell, with its UFO lure. I can't wait to get my share of souvenirs from the International UFO Museum and Research Center. It's the biggest tourist attraction in New Mexico. You know I can't wait to go there." "There's also Bandelier National Monument, which has archaeological

ruins of ancestral Pueblo people."

"We can view ancient drawings at the Petroglyph National Monument. The area is more than just a monument. It includes five dormant volcanoes, a large mesa, which is a flat-topped hill, and also has a basalt escarpment, which is fine-grain volcanic rock."

"We can see the Gila Cliff Dwellings National Monument, which is north of Silver City, an old mining town. This park has hot springs, and old cliff homes of the Mogollon culture, Native Americans who lived in the southwest."

"Taos ski valley is beautiful. Just think, we can learn to ski right here in New Mexico."

"We can also see Taos, and the Taos Pueblo. That Pueblo, with its adobe structures, is over one thousand years old, and is still home of the Pueblo Indians."

"Pecos National Historical Park was once the largest native American Pueblo Indian community in New Mexico. It also holds a civil war battlefield."

"Chaco Culture National Historic Park is another site with more Pueblo Indian ruins. It is a UNESCO World Heritage Site. I'm sure you know UNESCO stands for the United Nations Educational, Scientific and Cultural Organization, which is a part of the United Nations, and has a mission of promoting world peace and security through education, arts, sciences, and culture."

"We will certainly visit Santa Fe many times, with its Pueblo-style architecture and museums."

"There's Chimayo, about thirty miles north of Santa Fe, where there's Santuario de Chimayo, a Roman Catholic church village hundreds of years old. It is a national historic landmark. It receives over two hundred and fifty thousand visitors every year. People from all over the world come for healing."

"Yeah, I'll bet there's healing there," Matt interrupted in a sarcastic tone. "Sure, there's healing!" she quickly responded. "It is said people go there on crutches and wheelchairs and leave healed, leaving their crutches and wheelchairs at the mission. There's healing because God heals, just like Jesus healed the sick and afflicted when He walked the earth." Matt kept the disagreement going.

"You can't claim that because you didn't see it. I'll say that I firmly believe in the power of suggestion of the mind, but I wouldn't call it miracle healing. The brain is very powerful, as you know. And I want our jobs to explore more of the power and potential of the brain, including making and using artificial intelligence."

"I believe in miracle healing," she responded.

"And I expect to perform miracle healing just like Jesus." Matt rolled his eyes. "Anyway," she continued, "let me finish talking about New Mexico attractions. There's Sandia Mountain, outside of Albuquerque, with the world's longest tram to the top. There's the black rock terrain of El Malpais, which was created by volcanos over millions of years. The Jemez valley land north of Albuquerque is very scenic. New Mexico has canyons, mountains, and forests. There is a lot more than the dry state most people think of when they think of New Mexico."

"Well, Ms. New Mexico expert," Matt quipped as the server placed their food order on the table.

"You didn't mention Fort Sumner." "What's Fort Sumner?"

"Fort Sumner is home of the Billy the Kid Museum," he answered. "And it is near where Sheriff Pat Garrett supposedly killed the Kid in eighteen eighty-one."

"The museum has an assortment of various artifacts and relics from that time period and later, including Billy the Kid's rifle, other antique guns and knives, stage coaches, calvary swords, antique cars, and of course a gift shop."

"It takes at least an hour to see and appreciate the museum. My dad took me there when I was ten, and I want to go back and take you there. I want to go as soon as we can. You know I'm such an avid follower of the American west and those villains and heroes of the time when the west was really wild."

"The only thing I don't do anymore is ride horses. You know my story of the scar on my knee coming from falling off a horse when the horse started galloping. I was only five when my dad took me horseback riding. He told me to hold on, but I didn't hold on tight enough."

"But first things first. This weekend I've got to find a golf course. It has been a while since I played golf, with all of our moving and transitioning." "And I'm afraid I'm going to be terrible. I have to play often to keep

up what little golf skill I have. I can only break ninety-five if I play on a regular basis. It's so hard just breaking a hundred. Ninety five percent of the world's amateur golfers don't break a hundred without cheating or using their own rules."

"I plan to join a private country club here to make some upper-crust playing buddies. But I also want to play regular golf courses to have some real friends."

"Golf is my one vice. I have to blame my dad for that. I say 'blame,' because golf is so hard. I know it looks easy, but it can be more frustrating than gratifying. It's the only thing I have undertaken without a satisfying level of success. I know I have to really put my mind to it."

"Okay, you and your golf."

"Maybe I'll take up the game one day. But I still want you to have your 'me' time with your buddies. What I really want is you to teach me how to shoot guns."

"I know you want me to teach you martial arts skills. And I want to be even more self-assured and protected by learning to shoot guns."

"But with all of this planning, remember in three weeks your dad is coming. And next month we visit my parents."

"Now let's enjoy this good-looking meal. But first I need to pray over our food."

"Okay, okay," he relented.

Two hours later, after they ate and drove around town, they arrived back at their house and walked through the door. They hugged again and looked around the spacious living room. Then Tangie spoke.

"This is a dream come true. We have so much to be thankful for." She then paused and stepped back as a serious look came over her face.

"Matt, I know we plan to slowly work on the things we differ on, but I feel compelled by the Holy Spirit to get you saved as soon as possible."

"You never know when something could happen, and then you won't have another opportunity to accept Jesus as your Lord and Savior."

"Holy Spirit?" he asked, looking for further explanation.

"Yes, the Holy Spirit. The Godhead is three persons; the Father, God; Jesus; and the Holy Spirit. The Holy Spirit comes to live in you when you are saved. He helps you deal with the evils of this world."

"You know the world is cursed with evil because the devil and his demons are here seeking who he can destroy and turn against God."

"The Holy Spirit helps with doing good things such as healing. I can't wait to visit orphanages, hospitals, and the sick to use God's healing powers and fight the devil."

"I believe I haven't been sick a day in my life because of His healing power. Jesus released those healing powers two thousand years ago when He died on the cross. All we have to do is accept the healing."

"Wait! Wait!" he raised his voice, as he walked around the room stroking his fingers through his thick head of hair.

"This is too much too soon. You are overwhelming me with all of this holy moly stuff. You are giving me answers that I have questions for. I think it will work better if I ask the questions first in the order that I need to try to understand them."

"Okay," she responded, as she wanted him to calm down and was relieved at his willingness to listen, at least at his pace.

"I know some things in the Bible," he said in a calmer tone.

"I have heard them, and my mother read the Bible. She was very spiritual. But the stuff mainly confused me. You know how I think, and how the brain works. Things have been logical to me."

"And the religions practiced today are so different that I don't know which is the right one."

He continued, "For instance, I want to know where your God came from. I want to understand how He can see and hear all the people of the earth at the same time. Why do some people dress the way they do to go to church or perform religious ceremonies?"

"I have a lot of these confusing types of questions."

"Okay," she responded as they sat down on a sofa in the room.

"Good and fair questions. Let me first clear things up about church rituals and ceremonies. All you need to do to go to heaven is accept and believe in Jesus. None of the other stuff is necessary. Most of those are not even in the Bible. Jesus Himself says in the Bible that man let those traditions get in the way of the true word of God."

"You know I will be looking in this town for a nondenominational church because what you wear to church, what ritual you perform, or how many Christian artifacts you have has nothing to do with going to heaven or not. And many religions have their own interpretations. And there are a lot of false prophets out there."

"Many people, even devout Christians, believe and practice much stuff that is passed down through generations. And some Christian churches don't even teach many parts of the Bible."

"And many still believe and practice many laws or traditions of the Old Testament. But we live under the New Testament, a new Covenant that Jesus and Saint Paul came to teach and spread all over the world."

"I bet you believe people who worship the devil and practice witchcraft are like you, but to the contrary. They actually study the Bible so they better know what they need to fight against."

"I'm glad you at least acknowledge the Bible. It is the greatest history book ever written. But many people believe the Bible is fictional."

"I know you study world history. Look at how Biblical history mirrors the history of cultures and civilizations you studied in history classes."

"Look at the Roman Empire, the Egyptian Empire, the Babylonian Empire."

"Look at cultures like the Assyrians, the Hittites, the Samarians, the Philistines."

"Look at bodies of water like the Tigris, Euphrates, Jordan, and Nile rivers. The Red Sea. The Sea of Galilee."

"Look at archeological ruins like the ancient cities of Nineveh, Babylonia, Petra, the Ruins of Rome. Look at the artifacts of the people and cultures mentioned in the Bible."

"Look at the ancient rulers, not just the kings of Jerusalem and Judah, but other leaders like the Egyptian Pharaohs, Caesar and Pontius Pilate of Rome and King Nebuchadnezzar of Babylon."

"If people know these people and places exist or existed, why do they not believe Jesus lived?"

"One thought I want you to carry as we journey through this marriage, our careers, and through life. Why take a chance on being a nonbeliever?" "If you're going to take a chance, why not choose to believe, like me?

If I'm wrong, then when we die, we're just gone, and there's no afterlife. But at least my belief led me to live a better life helping people and trying to be a good person."

"But if I'm right, when we die, I go to heaven and live forever. Nonbelievers go to hell and are tormented in a lake of fire forever. Why take a chance on being wrong?"

"That's a fair way to look at it," Matt responded. "I'll give you that point. And we will have plenty of banter on this subject."

"But right now, we need to go to bed and get a good night's sleep. We have a very interesting day tomorrow."

"Okay," she relented. "We do need some rest. But first I need to call my parents."

"And I need to call my dad," Matt said. "And I also need to call my man Julius."

7

FIRST DAY ON THE JOB

"Time to roll!" Matt exclaimed the next morning, as he rolled over and shut off the alarm clock.

Tangie rose up and responded. "Let's do it!"

They showered and dressed and headed out on the road to Carlsbad Caverns. Matt placed his cell phone in a phone holder on the car dash-board, as they awaited instructions.

After five minutes a noise came on the phone. It started with a series of beeps that lasted for a few seconds, then a long and loud screeching sound that lasted five seconds.

"Drive past the visitor's center to the fenced parking lot. The gate will open for you. Walk to the building at the end of the parking lot. Scan the numbers that will appear on your phone. Enter the elevator after you enter the building." Ten seconds after the voice stopped, a series of numbers started clicking up on the phone.

They did as told. They entered an elevator at the back of the building. After ten seconds the elevator stopped. A door opened in front of them. Standing directly in front of them was a man dressed in a black suit.

"Mr. and Mrs. Riley, welcome to G.O.D." the man called, with outstretched arms.

"My name is Harold Flundy. Please walk through the scanner."

They looked around at the circle atrium behind the man. They walked through a scanner that encircled them. They could see themselves being scanned in four dimensions.

The atrium was about the size of a football field. There were five metal doors around the circumference of the atrium. The doors were labeled Level 1 through Level 5.

"Nice to meet you, Mr. Flundy," they said as they shook his hand. "Very interesting entrance to your establishment," Matt said in mild

amazement. "Well," he said, "as they say, you ain't seen nothing yet. Please follow me," he commanded in a businesslike tone as he led them to an office next to the first level door. He held his left pinky finger up to a scanner on the door, and the door opened.

"Please have a seat," he commanded.

He pointed to the two chairs in front of a large desk, and then walked around the desk and sat down in his seat. Behind him was a large three-dimensional flat world map display, with various cities and other points around the globe highlighted with red dots. Yellow lines connected the various points.

Directly across the room on the wall was a large screen with a three-dimensional human brain. The various physical parts of the brain were labeled on the screen.

"I'll get straight to the point," he continued.

"We know enough about you to skip the small talk, orientations, physicals, training tests, probations, and all that new job stuff. You were chosen because of your intellectual abilities, and we want to tap those abilities. We have many things we want you to do regarding artificial intelligence, chemical composition, metaphysical expansion, and military applications of the human brain."

"Almost all studies, experiments, tests, and theories of mind control involved drugs, implants, or devices of some sort, where you have to actually touch the person, have them take medications, or use a device."

"We believe there is a way to read the brain, not only in humans, but also animals, and control brain functions without actually having the subjects' participation or presence."

"Specifically, we believe you two can crack the code of reading and controlling the brain, and thus improve the human mind to be able to develop and apply much better products and applications of the areas I just mentioned. And we believe it can be done without using any kind of drugs or devices. That's what this program is all about."

"The possibilities are endless, given the potential of the brain. You can make computers and phones obsolete."

"The brain has the ability to command the body to heal itself, thus eliminating the need for dependency on medicines. Think of how much more curing you could bring to the world."

"The brain controls emotions. If you can control emotions, you can prevent conflicts. You can control a person's desire to go to war, or control the other side's willingness to fight back. Think of how much more peace you would bring to the world."

"You two are the perfect people to help achieve our goals. You haven't worked for any other organization that could condition your minds or initiate practices that could restrict or limit your creativity, imagination, and methodologies."

"We believe telepathy and extra-sensory perception are very real and usable senses. We believe you have the ability to develop and apply those senses to the parts of the brain that receives and makes commands to emotions and physical actions."

"You are outside the boxers who need to continue thinking outside the box. We provide the tools, guidance, and motivation to allow you to apply your enormous potential."

"This facility is New Mexico's version of Nevada's Area Fifty One, but without the publicity. Doing work for the progress of America, and thus the betterment of the world."

"We reside here in the off-limits section of Carlsbad Caverns. You saw the five doors of this facility. You both will work in Level One until your supervisor believes you are ready to go to the next level."

"Then you will go to Level Two. Levels One and Two are where we expect you will do more for us than we are doing for you. You will only understand that when you advance to those levels."

"When we get what we need from you on those levels, you will be granted security clearance to Level Four. I have to tell you not many people make it to Levels Four and Five. I have faith that both of you will pass the requisite accomplishments to advance to those levels. You two have impressive histories of success and never giving up."

"What about Level Three.?" Matt asked.

"We'll talk about Level Three later on." Mr. Flundy answered.

"It goes without saying you will tell no one exactly what you do or where you work. Your cover to the average person will be that you work on secret projects for Los Alamos."

"You are hereby sworn to secrecy the rest of your lives. If you are ever interrogated, you tell them you work for God, and you will pass the polygraph."

"You are being paid out of an international bank that handles funds for covert operations around the world. We are not funded by some federal government black-box budget."

"Our CIA and some levels of our military are aware of our operation. We report to them. But this is a secret operation, and we are fairly free to operate without a high level of scrutiny. We expect you will go further than just stare at goats."

"If you decide to opt out of the jobs, that time is today. Here's your folders with further rules and policies of the job."

He handed each of them green strapped folders.

"That's all I need you for today," he concluded, as he stood up and pointed to the office door.

"Be back here Monday morning. You will be given the code to get through security on your phone when you come Monday. The code changes every day."

"Well, what's behind curtain number one?" Matt snidely asked as they got back into their car.

"The plot thickens."

CHAPTER

8

THE NEXT DAY

Saturday evening, Matt returned from golfing. "How did it go?" Tangie asked in an upbeat tone.

"I was terrible!" Matt exclaimed, with a tired and discouraged response, as he threw his golf bag into the corner of the living room.

"I knew I would be rusty since I haven't played in months, and I went to the driving range to try to get my swing back. But when I played it was like I was playing golf for the first time or never took lessons. I shot one hundred ten, and wanted to throw my clubs away."

"My dad was better than I will ever be. I am not able to apply any scientific analytics to improve. It's more about practicing and focusing."

"Well," she responded. "Think about the positive things that happened today, and go from there."

"The only positive I got from today was that I met a couple of guys that I plan to play with," he answered as he headed to the kitchen to grab a cold beverage.

"Keep at it," she encouraged, as she followed him into the kitchen.

"I'm glad you already found some golfing buddies. When will you be golfing with them again?"

"I think in a couple weeks," he answered as he pulled a bottled water from the refrigerator.

"I got their names, Clark Mann and Greg Dugan. Mr. Mann is a CPA, and Mr. Dugan is a teacher. Both are in their late forties, and have been playing golf for years. They shoot in the low eighties, and many times in the seventies."

"I got their business cards. I told them I'm a research scientist, and that Los Alamos has many projects. That was enough for them, and we turned our attention back to golf."

"They had two other playing partners, who came down from Albuquerque and played with them. They said these guys were also secretive about what they did. So, they are used to playing with people who they don't know much about what they do for a living. Guess that's the culture when you have places like Los Alamos in the state. This is the state where the atomic bomb was conceived under a lot of secrecy."

"I need to practice some more. I was playing by myself. They were ahead of me and asked me to play with them."

"Most people like to play with their buddies and don't usually let anybody into their golfing routine, but these two guys are part of a foursome, and their other golfing buddies have not played with them recently, and were not able to play today, so I guess they are used to playing with more than two people."

"But they were very open to having a foursome. They mentioned that when they play on Saturday mornings when most golf courses have foursomes playing, they are often asked to let other people play with them when those people come out to play as a single. Most singles that come out during busy times expect that they will be paired with other golfers. But those guys said they would rather have another two regulars than play with some of the characters they have to play with. They were excited to know that I plan to be a regular there."

"By the way, how did your day go?" "Very well."

"I was busy online and on the phone. I found a nondenominational church that I plan to attend tomorrow. They have white, black, and Hispanic members attending. That's what I was looking for; a church that looks like what heaven looks like."

"I also found a karate studio. It's not too far from here. And I checked on a gun shooting range for us."

"Great!" he responded and clapped his hands.

Her eyes lit up with his positive body language. "You know, we're gonna need a second car for our separate extracurricular activities. We're gonna combine more of our activities, and I know you will attend church with me at some point, but we still need another car for our 'me' time activities and events."

"Yeah," he agreed.

"We will start stopping by dealerships after work. I know you're the SUV type, and it will be an EV."

"Yes," she chimed in.

"I believe in your spare time you can help the EV industry by developing a battery that gets much more miles to the charge than today's autos." "I'm not an engineer," he responded. "I'm a scientist. But the idea of developing a much longer lasting car battery sounds intriguing. And I'll set up a workshop in our garage, as well as a workout gym in our spare bedroom." "Dad had me working on cars. That was another one of his hobbies.

It would be good to get back into that again."

"And we'll get a dog pretty soon. We'll have to decide which kind. You know I like German Shepherds and Collies. You like Golden Retrievers."

"Yes, a doggie." she added, then struck a more serious tone.

"You know what? All of our family and friends have basically looked at us as perfect all of our lives. There has not been a perfect person in the history of man except Jesus Christ."

"I know things have gone really well for us, and we have been gifted with a high intellect."

"But we're not perfect. I never use that word about myself. I rather use the word 'blessed.'"

"No, we're not perfect," he added.

"My golf game is a testament to that. And I got a feeling the first few months on our jobs will make us feel like a lost ball in high weeds. And it is still to be determined if we can make the contributions to the industry and the world that our employer and even, we ourselves believe we will make."

CHAPTER

9

MONDAY MORNING

"I wonder if Mr. Flundy will be any more user friendly today than he was Friday." Tangie quipped, as the two of them stepped into the elevator to go down into the research complex.

"Well," Matt responded, "this is serious and secret work we are doing. I don't expect there will be many coworkers we will be socializing with just because of the nature of our jobs."

As the elevator door opened, standing there to greet them was a middle-age African American woman with a bright smile.

"Welcome, Rileys!" she called out with open arms as they walked through the body scanner.

"My name is Flora Grace, but please just call me Flo." She shook their hands vigorously, and they looked at each other with the look that they knew in their minds they were thinking; *'This is certainly not Mr. Flundy!'* "Please follow me to Level One." She swiveled and walked to the Level

1 door. She held up her pinky finger to the scanner. The door opened. Then she continued talking.

"We are very excited to have you two here. We have been anxiously awaiting y'all to come on board. I heard you two will be able to take us to the next level in cognitive psychology."

They walked through with her, looking around at numerous models and labels of the human brain. They also saw a real human brain in a liquid substance.

They expected to see other people.

"You're the only people I will be working with. There's not a lot of people like you, and not a lot of people work here." They sat down at one of the lab tables, and she continued talking.

"I can't tell you everything about this place. All I can do is prepare y'all for Level Two. We're not exactly sure when you will be ready for Level Two, but it's my job to prepare you, and I will know when you're ready."

"I'm a neuroscientist, or in other words, a brain scientist. I love human science, and studying the human brain. I have undergraduate degrees in biology, psychology, and molecular engineering."

"I love to learn about physical and mental behavior. I have mastered meditation techniques."

"I have a PhD in Neuroscience. My thesis was on the untapped potential in the human brain, and what we could achieve if we accessed that potential. I theorized that the human mind is the best computer on earth, and could replace computers if we unlock more of our brain's potential." "Like you guys, I have all kinds of scholastic honors. And I'm a certified hypnotist."

"How did you wind up here?" Tangie asked.

"This place came out of nowhere twenty-five years ago and scooped me up. The money was so good I didn't ask questions. Y'all know how good the money is here. I have been able to live my dreams."

"I started an orphanage in Paradise Hills, a suburb of Albuquerque. It serves many good causes. It's an orphanage for parentless kids. It's a rescue shelter from human trafficking. We treat drug addiction. It's doing very well." "We have a chapel. We now receive donations from all over the world.

I named it Grace and Peace."

"That sounds fantastic!" Matt said with excitement.

"Those things are so near and dear to our hearts. We want to do more than just donate money to good causes."

"Maybe y'all can come up and visit soon." Flo responded.

"We'd love to do that." Tangie added, then asked, "What kind of religion do you practice?"

"Well, I don't have a denomination.

"I don't have a denomination. I grew up in a Baptist church, but moved away because I was more of a non-traditionalist. I didn't exactly enjoy being expected to save and wear my best dresses to church. And I was never much of a fan to the hollering and shouting they do in many of those churches. Those things weren't exactly what I thought church should emphasize, just the word of God."

"My sentiments exactly!" Tangie responded.

"And I believe I have found a good nondenominational church." "Good for y'all!" Flo said.

"It's not y'all yet," Tangie returned.

"I'm still working on Matt. He's more of a nonbeliever, but I just have to get him convinced."

"We'll just have to get him convinced. And I'm proud to tell people I work for God," Flo added then continued, "Anyway, I'm sure you two can cite all the parts and functions of the brain and the central nervous system in your sleep."

"You know the functions and positions of the brain lobes and cerebellum, and what each area controls. You know what the right side and left side of the brain does. This is not a basic Brain 101 class."

"This is more theoretical, conceptual training. My job is to build on your knowledge about the brain, and turn that knowledge into avenues, concepts, and real applications about the possibilities of the brain."

"We need to open your minds to brain communication, and how one function can interact with or even control another function. We will concentrate how the brain communicates with itself, and how that communication can transmit to the rest of the body."

"We need to strengthen your ability, for instance, to interact right side creativity with left side analysis, and then take it to physical action at a higher level than what is considered normal."

"I know you are aware that a Spanish scientist named Jose Delgado used a radio transmitter planted in a bull's brain and controlled that bull's behavior by stopping the bull from charging at the matador."

They nodded their heads with an affirmative 'Yes'.

"I'm sure you know about savants who can perform computer fast calculations in their minds."

"You know about humans who can perform incredible feats of physical strength when they find themselves in a critical situation."

"You know the stories about monks and others who can levitate or bend objects without touching the objects."

"Y'all know about secret government programs on UFOs, mind altering, and mind control not just here in the United States, but China, Russia, and other countries."

"The United States had a black budget for such programs. Many of the known programs discontinued in public form, but I believe many continued in a secret way."

"I don't know what the goals are of the people on Level Five. I just pray they are working for peace."

"My job is to get you two to fully believe those types of things can be done by anyone."

"My job is to train you to find the avenue whereby the average person can learn to do those things and much more."

"You will learn and experiment in ways to get people to use their own minds to solve problems."

"You will figure out how to get the brain to send the right signals, not just to the right nerves and receptors to learn or get things done, but to also send signals to itself so that the normal signal becomes an exponent of itself." "In other words, you can train the brain to become a super computer and do it without any drugs. I believe the brain can send signals to strengthen and direct its own signals. And I believe you two can prove it." "We do no physical experiments or specimen examinations on this level. This level is purely based on improving brain knowledge and inter-

action though cognitive and theoretical learning and exercises."

"They don't choose mentalists, psychics, clairvoyants, diviners, mediums, prophets, seers, telepathists, spiritualists, fortune tellers, soothsayers, voodooist, buddhas, savants, drug addicts, or drug-dependent people for this assignment. Those people already have mind conditions that can't be unlearned. And they have their own preconceived motivations, plans, and limits on what they can be taught."

"You two are basically empty vessels just waiting to be filled in the right way."

"Why haven't they asked you to do those things they want us to accomplish instead of just teaching people how to do it?" Matt asked.

"Listen," she answered. "I'm comfortable doing what I do. I don't know and don't want to know what goes on in Level Four or Level Five."

"I don't know who's in those chambers. I just take their orders."

"I sent two men to Level Two about two years ago. I don't know if they made it any further. I don't see them. I don't see many people. This is a secret facility. I believe not many people know or need to know everything about this place."

"I don't even think many government officials know about this place." "I personally don't believe they want me to work on any higher levels because I bring my Bible to work, and they probably think I will try to influence or save people. Being a brain factory, they probably believe that

will interfere with their work."

"I pray for them, and I know God always sends me to the right people for me to work with. We should never try to force our Christianity on people."

"Amen," Tangie agreed.

Flo continued, "A man who worked in Level Four came down to visit with me a couple of times, and took me to Level Four."

"He was nice. He gave me this magnetic looking piece, and asked me to see if I could analyze it."

She picked a small metallic object from a nearby table. The object looked like a black automobile engine spark plug.

"And he said he felt compelled to give it to me for proper analysis. But not long after that he was gone."

"They must not have known what he did with it, because they never came and asked me about it. They probably didn't know that he visited me." "He said they have many unknown objects in there. So maybe they were so busy with other things that he wanted me to check this one out." "I've secretly had the object analyzed at the University of New Mexico. They haven't found any known metallic compound that makes up this thing."

"I've just kept it and waited for the right time to give it back or give it to people who may be able to figure it out."

She handed the object to Matt.

"Doesn't look like anything I've seen before in any of my automotive or chemistry work," Matt said.

"Me either," Tangie added.

Matt handed the object back to Flo.

"It was given to me for a reason. Maybe not to be used, but to prove a point. I kept it to keep me grounded. To let me know there's always another challenge. We don't know everything."

"The Bible says in the book of Deuteronomy that the secret things belong to God. So, this reminds me that I can't always learn everything I want to learn."

"With that, let's close the day."

"Y'all know the human brain can only absorb so much in a certain span of time for that information to be effective. We've had enough for today." "See y'all tomorrow. We don't work eight hours. Some days it may

be more, some days it may be less. The brain works differently each day." "One more thing," Flo exclaimed as the pair stood up and turned to leave. "I'm retiring when I get you two through this training. I'm ready to

relax and enjoy helping people who really need help." "Congratulations!" both of them replied back to her.

Then Matt added. "We'll do what we can to get you to your grace and peace as soon as possible."

"As a matter of fact," Tangie added, "there's a lot of places in New Mexico we want to visit, but we want to visit you there as soon as we can." "I'll be very happy to have y'all anytime," Flo exclaimed, with a big smile.

"I'll put y'all to work."

10

NINE MONTHS LATER – GRADUATION AND RETIREMENT

" It's time for you two to graduate and move on to Level Two," Flo said to the pair as they came in on Monday morning.

"I believe you both have expanded your brainpower to the point that you are conditioned to learn anything there is to learn in this world. You have passed all of the mental exercises with flying colors. You have solved equations. You have provided perspectives at PhD and higher levels. You have made logical conclusions that appeared outside the box that you made fit. You have mastered meditations. I believe your minds have expanded to another level. There is nothing else I can do for you. You two finished this training faster than anyone has done previously before you."

"We had a great teacher," Tangie responded, as she and Matt gave Flo a big embrace.

"You both will be in Level Two. I got a message that they are combining

Levels Two and Three into Level Two and letting men and women work together. I never saw a woman go through here, so I was not sure if they even used Level Three."

"I firmly believe God sent you two here for a reason, and you will accomplish the goals the important people have for you. I don't know who will take over after me. As you already know, this place is very secretive." "Thursday will be the last day for y'all to work in Level One. I will come in Friday and clean out my office. By Thursday I'll program your fingerprints for entry to enter Level Two."

"There's one more thing," Flo said as she turned and picked up the object the worker on Level 4 had given her.

"I want y'all to take this," she said, as she handed the object to Matt. "There's something about this thing that I believe you two will figure out."

11

GRADUATION WEEKEND

S aturday morning the couple ate breakfast.

"You know, after nine months our jobs are still shrouded in mystery." Tangie said, as she dug her spoon into a grapefruit half.

"We have no idea what Monday is going to be like."

"Yeah," Matt replied, as he poured a glass of milk from a jug at the refrigerator.

"But that is kind of what we expected, and there's no reason to believe things will change."

"Mister Flundy said that we would be involved in all kinds of sciences, research, and experiments. I believe they expect a lot from us. Just hope we can deliver. This is kind of cool."

"I sorta feel like we are independent contractors. According to our benefits package, we can take off whenever we want, although it seems like the whole place is depending on our intellects."

"I don't want to do things that are immoral," she responded. "But if we are contributing to the benefit of mankind, I'm all in." "Work is a bit of a mystery," he responded.

"But everything else is falling in place. Our families love our home. And they accept the fact that we can't discuss our jobs. Almost seems like they expected that. Even our old and new friends accept our job secrecy." "You're happy with your church. And looks like your spiritual walk is increasing."

"Your martial arts classes are going well. And you're teaching me some good moves."

"You are getting very good with shooting guns at the shooting range.

I'll take full credit for that. Like you said, iron sharpens iron."

"We have visited some great places here in New Mexico; White Sands, Gila Cliff Dwellings, Petroglyph National Monument. This is a fascinating state."

"Not to mention visiting Flo's orphanage. She is doing great work. I'm glad we signed up to make a nice monthly contribution to help her run her facility. As our jobs settle, we can go and actually get our hands dirty helping out."

"Yes," Tangie responded.

"Things are going well, but not everything has fallen in place."

"You still haven't attended church with me, although I expect you will." "I may be getting close to meeting your wish," he answered.

"I'm still open to trying to see if I can figure out this Christian and faith stuff. I'm such a pragmatist that going with a lot of what I can't see and feel is very difficult for me."

"I know," she returned.

"But I have that blind faith that you will come around, and things will make rational sense to you."

"And I can't believe we haven't visited Fort Sumner yet." "Soon," he answered.

"And when we go, we can come back through Roswell."

"There is another thing that is not well, at least not well with me. My golfing game is not improving as much as I expect. I just can't figure that out. I'm practicing as much as I can, but I still can't break ninety on a regular basis. Too many mistakes."

"But I enjoy playing with Clark and Greg. They have accepted me, especially since their other golfing buddy died of cancer. They play much better than I do, but they are patient with me, and are very encouraging."

"I'm looking forward to playing today, while you attend your yoga class. I'm glad we now incorporate yoga based on Flo's recommendation." "And speaking of taking time off, we need to start planning our Tahiti vacation."

They finished their breakfast.

Tangie pulled her car keys off the key rack and turned to Matt. "Even though we don't yet have any children, it's a good thing we

bought a second car," she said.

"We have so many different things to do at the same time, usually on the weekends. And I love my electric SUV."

"Yeah," he agreed.

"And I'm enjoying learning how an EV operates. I grew up working on gas engines."

"I love it," she added.

"But I wish the battery lasted longer. And it would be great if it didn't take so long to recharge. It doesn't even last as long as they say it should last when I have the AC or heat on full blast."

"Maybe I will start working on a new battery." Matt said in a bit of a sarcastic tone.

CHAPTER

12

LEVEL 2

"Welcome Matt, welcome Tangie, to Level Two," a voice sounded off as the Level 2 door closed behind them. They looked around. There was no one in the room.

The room was a 50 x 100-foot rectangle enclosure. There was nothing in the room except a small table and two chairs. The walls were full of many different size square and rectangle compartment doors.

Most of the doors were small, of one foot by one foot in size. Some were one foot by three feet. But two walls had two doors about the size of a regular house door.

On another wall was a screen with a touchpad.

The couple assumed that things would come out of the walls for them to use and work with.

The voice continued, "Congratulations on graduating to Level Two. You two have mastered many brain functions to the point that we believe you can train your brains to perform many and most of the things the human brain is capable of doing."

"Once you perform the duties at this level, you will advance to Level Four for practical brain applications."

"In this room you will NEVER, I repeat NEVER, speak in this room, or write any messages to each other."

"Drink only water and milk to help your brain's cognitive process." "Eat mainly fruits, vegetables, and meat full of proteins. No bread.

No alcohol."

"Your lunch will be served to you each day. It will come to you from the food compartment at the back of the room."

"Take no vitamins, as most vitamins have additional ingredients that can interfere with your thinking process."

"When you communicate with each other in this room, it will only be with an affirmative nod for 'YES' and a negative shake of the head for 'NO.'"

"At the end of each day you will input all the information and results of your day into the console rectifier on the wall. You will make no writ- ten notes. You will always self-encode and self-encrypt your information so that no one can hack into your systems. Each day you will change and memorize your encryption steps."

"Now, we are going to get right into your training. Your rate of progress depends on you."

One of the compartments slid open and out came a small tray with a deck of playing cards. The voice continued, "Matt, take the cards, and both of you sit at the table facing each other."

They took their seats.

The voice continued, "Matt, shuffle the cards for ten seconds, and hold the cards facing you."

He did as commanded.

"Tangie, look into Matt's eyes and tell him without speaking which card you want him to place face up on the table. Nod your head to him when you have decided which card you want him to lay down."

Tangie thought for five seconds and pictured the queen of clubs in her mind. She nodded to Matt.

Matt placed the 8 of hearts on the table. Tangie shook her head for "NO."

"Do it again!" the voice commanded.

They repeated the exercise for the remainder of the day without matching Tangie's thought with Matt's card selections.

The next day, the voice greeted them as soon as the door closed. "Since you two failed the task yesterday, it will be repeated again today." "Matt, make sure you take your time to receive the telepathic communication from Tangie. There is no time limit for you to receive her command, process that command, and then select the card she has ordered you to select."

"And Tangie, since there is only a fifty-two-to-one chance Matt will select the card you are thinking of, you will think of the same card many times, even thinking of the same card again before you think of the entire deck of cards."

The two repeated the task all the second day without any success.

The following Monday, they entered the room and was greeted by the voice.

"Today Tangie will hold the cards, and Matt will command which card she selects."

They performed the task all that day, and all week without a match. The next week they were greeted by the voice.

"Matt, you will hold the cards again."

"Are you expressing frustration at home about failing to match each other's thoughts?"

They both nodded an affirmative YES.

"Then you are failing the task. Not failing yet at matching cards, but failing at controlling your emotions of not being able to telepath your card commands. That brain function is interfering with your ability to communicate brain thoughts to each other."

"When you can reach down into your brains and get in touch with those parts that receive thoughts and emanate emotions, you will be in a better position to talk to each other without actually talking."

"I think I get it," Matt exclaimed, as the two strapped into their car to drive home that evening.

"Yes!" Tangie agreed.

"We obviously have a ways to go with learning the entire thinking process, and how all of it relates," Matt spoke back.

"Yeah. All of our relaxation and meditation have not helped us yet because we did not use or connect it to every situation."

"Let's add getaways to our relaxation and emotion control. Let's go to Fort Sumner and Roswell this weekend."

"Sounds good to me, but don't forget the Hudsons from church invited us to dinner Friday night."

CHAPTER

13

THE ABDUCTION

"You said the tour of this Billy The Kid museum would take about an hour," Tangie said to Matt as they stepped out of the museum door and headed to their car in the museum parking lot.

"We've been here all day, and I thoroughly enjoyed it. I learned so much. I got chills when I saw Billy the Kid's actual rifle."

"Yeah," Matt added.

"We both got caught up with the artifacts and history of this place and the area. This is my kind of place."

"It's so late now that it will be dark when we get to Roswell. We may as well stay the night there and see it tomorrow."

They got in their car and drove onto Route 20 heading southwest to Roswell. It was close to sundown when they rode out of Fort Sumner and onto Route 20.

"This road is so straight it can cause highway hypnosis," Matt said, as he drove into the setting sun."

"But I think I can stay alert for eighty-five miles." "I hope so," she responded.

"Because it's probably not much to see to keep you alert on a straight road. Just desert and darkness. Probably not many cars."

As darkness overtook them, Matt looked into his rearview mirror and saw a light approaching from behind.

"Looks like we may have some company out here. There's a light coming up behind us," he said, as Tangie awoke from dosing off.

"Might be an ambulance," she said as she looked back.

"It's approaching real fast, and the light looks very bright. I wonder where they are going. There's not much out here. It kind of looks like it's up in the sky coming down, but that may just be the optical illusion of this straight road and this time of night."

She turned back around as they expected the light to pass their car. The next moment, Matt opened his eyes and came out of a bit of a trance. He lay halfway up in a type of a bed stretcher. Pulsating red, white, and green straps about an inch in diameter were around his calfs, thighs, torso, lower arms, upper arms, and his forehead.

In an instant he realized alien beings existed, and that he and Tangie had been abducted.

Out of the corner of his eye to his right he could see a dim view of Tangie lying down, also strapped with colored pulsating straps. Two alien beings were on each side of her examining her.

The beings looked like one of what Matt had seen in pictures and descriptions of aliens. They were about five feet tall with long necks and large heads. They were grayish green in color, with small noses. They had no ears or mouths.

He turned his restrained head left as much as he could, and noticed two beings sitting and looking at him. It was a dim view, as the room was mostly dark, and the beings were not close to him, about fifteen feet away. The beings were slightly nodding their heads. Matt felt they were confirming their existence to him. He felt they were willing to communicate with him, not through talking, as they had no mouth, but through telepathic language. He felt they would answer any question he was willing to ask.

In his mind, he asked them, "Where did you come from?" They answered as their heads moved.

"We come from a solar system millions of light years from your Earth."

He asked several more questions with his mind, based on what he had seen, read, and heard about aliens and UFOs.

"How many of you are there on Earth?" "How did your civilization begin?" "Why do you look like you do?"

"How do your spacecrafts travel so fast?"

"How does your technology work compare to Earth technology?" "Where do you reside on Earth?"

"Are UFO crashes like the one reported near Roswell true UFO crash events?"

"Do you interact with man on Earth?" "What is your purpose on Earth?"

"What do you plan to do with my wife and me?"

The aliens starting to move their heads in a manner that made him feel they were going to answer his questions.

"There are thousands of us on your Earth. We have always been in existence. There are six different alien types that inhabit your Earth. That's why some look different than others, but all have much larger brains than you do, which makes us thousands of times more intelligent than even the smartest of mortals on your Earth."

They continued providing information.

"We come from millions of light years from your Earth. Some of our types used to inhabit the planet you call Mars, but over millions of years the planet became uninhabitable."

"We travel in crafts we designed and made in our galaxies, of material that does not age and is not a metal of any of your Earth's metals."

"You see six different types of crafts around your Earth because each of us have our own craft. Some are oval, belonging to that alien species. Some are triangular, belonging to that alien species. Some are what you would call cigar shaped, belonging to that species. Some are round, belonging to that species, and others change their shape."

"All of the aliens are not of the same level of technology. Some of those crafts are not as well designed to handle your Earth's atmosphere as well as others. That's why there are UFO crashes sometimes, like the one near Roswell, and other places."

"Other types of aliens are more advanced, can survive in your atmosphere, and even reside in your oceans as well as space. That is us. You have some of the less technology crafts captured in your Area Fifty One and other places."

"Some operate from the side of the moon away from your Earth. We all reside and operate from hidden and isolated places on your Earth, such as your oceans, your north and south poles, Alaska, Siberia, and other places on land where your human population is very low."

"Our technology is at least six million years ahead of your Earth technology. You will never catch up."

"Many of your UFO sightings happen around the world's military instillations because we want to keep up with your military capabilities to destroy each other. You cannot destroy us, but you can destroy each other." "We travel through space by a technology you may call Visioteleport.

Like your cameras, satellites, and space probes that can find and focus on objects and galaxies light years away, we can focus our finders on objects far away, and then quickly transport our crafts to that place without any gravitational or cosmic effects."

"Like you humans can focus your camera lenses on something and then zoom your sight in close on that object or area, we focus on a distant area of the cosmos then zoom to that area just like your zoom lenses."

"Some of our types have been able to infiltrate your human society, and become human while still communicating with their mothership command."

"Others of our type design and deploy spies such as your Bigfoot, Yeti, and other types of creatures around your Earth. You never find any waste from those creatures because they do not have to eat or drink."

"In your ancient times we interacted with your humans and helped them tremendously. We were their gods. They worshipped us. We helped them build many of the ancient structures you see today such as the structures on Easter Island, pyramids, temples, large drawings in South America, and other places. There is no way they could have built such structures without our help."

"Stonehenge in England, and other landing structures were built by those aliens who wanted to land on your surface and interact with your mortals."

"We helped ancient civilizations build structures, such as the pyramids, and use other natural places such as the Grand Canyon, as navigation points. We use many of those places, including the large carvings in Peru, as navigation points."

"We use the inner and outer magnetic fields of your Earth to power our spacecrafts. We have power stations in various place on your Earth, such as Alaska, and your poles."

"There were several civilizations on your Earth before the ones mentioned in your Biblical recording of your history."

"As your world came into the nineteenth century, man started moving away from working with us. Man became greedy, insecure, and afraid, driving us to hide more. They worked harder to prove that aliens did not exist. We tried things like unexplainable crop circles and other signs to prove and have man accept our existence, but your modern governments became even more determined to hide us."

"Your government had one of your United States presidents assassinated because he was planning to release information about the existence of aliens from other worlds. We were relegated to working with world governments in a secret way in secret places."

"America is our most interesting place to watch and study, because Americans are continually moving forward with technology, and have a no-limit attitude about good and bad possibilities in every aspect of human life."

"Like in the past, we work with your governments to help improve mankind on your Earth. Your global warming practices, wars, and other human rights abuses are destroying your Earth. We are trying to help you save yourselves from yourselves. We have the technology to help you improve. We need you to work with us to help make mankind and the physical world a better place to live."

"Your humans of the last two centuries have operated on politics, greed, selfishness, ignorance, and insensitivity. You could have had electric vehicles and many other technological improvements over one hundred years ago, but you let those human qualities get in the way. You are two hundred years behind where you should be technology wise in many communications, medical, social, financial, artificial intelligence, and mental aspects of historical growth because mortal man got in his own way."

"Although your mankind has made more technological strides in all areas of life within the past hundred and fifty years than over the previous time of human existence, you are not transparent about your progress."

"Most of your advancements come from studying and reverse engineering crashed alien crafts, and also secretly working with extraterrestrials in secret places."

"We have learned of you and where you work. We will send you back to use your intelligence to work for the good of mankind. And to make the world aware of how man really makes technological improvements."

Matt felt the beings were done releasing information. He started to drift off and lose consciousness.

While this went on with Matt, the aliens examined Tangie. She was terrified, as she laid strapped to a hospital-style bed.

One of the two beings with her put a mask over her mouth and nose. After about five seconds, she closed her eyes, and her head fell to the side as if she was knocked out by some type of nitrous oxide or another anesthetic. After a couple of minutes, she opened her eyes and looked straight up.

She could not turn her head to either side because the aliens had placed a collar around her neck that kept her head on one position. She was con-science that she was in a strange place, but was not sure if she had been abducted or if she was dreaming a lucid dream and experiencing sleep paralysis.

The aliens had placed a screen directly above her bed. She looked up at it, and the screen came on like a television. As the screen lit up, she was overcome with the feeling that she was in a dream that was going to show her events that were to take place in the future.

The first program panned over hundreds of homes and businesses destroyed in many places, as the pictures scanned over several southern states in the United States. She realized the damage was the result of many tornadoes that struct in clusters on the same day from a super storm.

She saw many first responders pulling dead victims out of destroyed homes. She saw videos of many towns flattened. She saw ambulances carrying hurt and dead people to many makeshift hospitals.

She saw a news reporter on the screen reporting about the damage. The caption under the reporter read "24,000 dead, 100,000 injured, 50,000 missing, as 30 tornadoes strike the southeast in historic superstorm."

The reporter introduced a witness who had captured one of the tornadoes as it destroyed a city in Alabama. The witness held up her device that showed debris flying as the two-mile wide tornado wiped an entire town off the map. There was a date on the screen of the device. She could not make out the entire date. She could only see the month and year, which was April 2064.

The screen then blanked off, and another event came on. It was a video of a gigantic geometric storm on the sun. A solar flare larger than any ever caught on telescopes flung away from the sun and hurled toward Earth. Tangie saw Chinese television reporting on the damage from the flare. The reporters showed video of completely dark cities in all of North America. They reported that all power and communication systems in that part of the world were knocked out when the flare reached Earth. They showed people looting and police arresting many looters all across America. She thought she saw a flash of the year on the video, which looked like 2117.

The screen turned to another scene, while Tangie continued believing that she was dreaming about future events.

The screen showed a nuclear explosion. The screen transitioned to a video of some people who appeared to be of Middle Eastern descent riding around in vehicles shooting their guns up in the air, apparently celebrating the explosion. The screen did not show the year.

The screen then flipped to another scene. It showed a woman in a bed in a hospital, giving birth to a baby. The doctor pulled the infant out of the womb slowly because the baby's head was larger than the usual baby's head. But the baby appeared healthy.

She saw the doctor extract the baby and then hand it over to another individual in the room.

"A nice, healthy American species," the doctor said, as he handed over the baby.

Tangie looked and saw the other individual in the room was an alien with a large head. The sight of the alien scared her to the point that she passed out.

When Matt and Tangie regained consciousness, they were back in their car, parked on the side of the road.

"I don't remember stopping to rest," Matt said as he shook his head and looked around.

"I guess we were more tired than we thought." Tangie said while yawning and raising her arms in the air. "It's a good thing you pulled over before you dozed off."

"Look at the time!" Matt exclaimed, as he looked at the car dashboard clock after he started the car.

"We left Fort Sumner around six o'clock. It's nearly eleven o'clock, and we are still forty-five minutes from Roswell. The entire drive from Fort Sumner to Roswell should take about an hour and a half. Two hours at the most. Five hours have passed."

"Well," Tangie said, "maybe we were more tired than we thought. You mentioned the highway hypnosis effect of driving on straight roads. I guess it's real, and we experienced it for the first time."

"Let's get to Roswell and find a hotel. And I won't miss church tomorrow. I will stream the service."

After the abduction, the two aliens that had been communicating with Matt communicated with each other.

The first one nodded to the second one and started to communicate to the second one telepathically.

"You know this is the most sophisticated chip we have ever implanted into a human. It will provide all the information about what he knows and learns about the GOD facility."

"It will also let us know his thoughts, everything he learns, and will pass on that technology to his children, their children, and their children, as well as all of the people he passes that knowledge on to."

"It will allow us to control their behavior and do our deeds on their Earth through their thoughts and actions."

"We will be able to take over the world and accomplish our goals." "The first thing on our list is to weed out and exterminate all those

do-good Christians."

"Then we will start a war between the two great superpowers." "America, and the world will be ours."

"We should have implanted it in her too," the second alien communicated.

"No," the first one answered.

"It is the first of its kind, and we want to study this first case by itself. And when it works as we designed, we won't need to do near as many abductions and implantations as we had been doing before now. The information transmitted from one person will be the same as twenty implantations in twenty different people."

"The implant should erase his memory of the abduction experience, even under their mortal hypnosis. But the information we provided him during the sedation time before he went out is in the memory section of his brain, but the chip should block access to that information."

"And he's such a healthy specimen that he should never feel the implant, especially since it is a nonmetallic biochip."

"The chip may also have some minor side effects on his physical or mental activities, but we don't expect there will be anything that bothers him or keeps us from accomplishing our mission."

"All humans seem to have some side effects from their abduction experiences. This implant is not only designed to prevent hypnotic regression in humans, but it is also designed to diagnose and prevent side effects from the implantation. That includes blocking nerve signals that are pain receptors or make muscles weak. So, the implant will make humans do much more than they would normally do, as well as providing the information to us that we desire."

14

BACK TO WORK, AND WEEKEND ACTIVITIES

Monday morning, the couple went back to work preparing the card command exercise. Tangie looked into Matt's eyes, thinking about the 8 of hearts card.

He looked into her eyes, then looked down at his cards. He pulled the 8 of hearts from the deck and laid it on the table. She nodded an affirmative "yes" to him, with a gleam in her eyes.

"Good work," the voice says. "Please repeat."

She then thought of the queen of clubs. He pulled the queen of clubs.

He pulled the correct club for the next two hours. "Change up now," the voice commanded.

Matt looked into Tangie's eyes, and was thinking of the ace of spades. She thought for a moment, then pulled the 3 of clubs. He shook his head for "No," and she looked disappointed. They repeated the exercise, but not matching each other's thoughts the rest of the day.

"You got this card exercise down now," Tangie said to Matt as they rode home after work.

"What do you think is working for you now?" "I don't know."

"Obviously the part of my brain that receives commands has picked up on your telepathic signals, and is working in sync with the part that controls recognizing and physical reaction."

"In other words, I think my temporal lobe, which processes auditory information, picked up your command in a telepathic manner, and transported that information to my frontal lobe, bypassing auditory senses. I was able to visualize the cards in my mind that you were thinking of."

"It felt like all brain functions were sitting ready to go all at the same time." "Whatever it is," she responded, "it's working for you."

On Thursday, Matt visually commanded Tangie to pick the 4 of diamonds. She placed the 4 of diamonds on the table. They both smiled after he nodded "yes" to her.

By Friday afternoon she had picked five cards correctly, but not every card he commanded. He correctly picked every card she commanded all week.

"We have made progress." the voice stated at the end of the day, and they were recording the information into the processing system.

"It is unusual for people to progress at the same rate. No two brains function exactly the same."

"Monday we will start a new exercise. I won't tell you about it, because I don't want you thinking about it over the weekend. I do want you thinking about future exercises so you can start training your brains for those exercises."

"In the coming months, you will break the Guinness world record for holding your breath. This exercise is to make sure your mental and physical performance are working together, and so that you can also be practicing this exercise."

"You will break the world record for the longest sequence of objects memorized."

"I will provide you some books to read and memorize."

"You will bring a musical instrument you do not play and learn how to play songs in record time."

"You will learn Mandarin Chinese in record time." "Have a good weekend."

Saturday morning, Matt met with Clark and Greg to play a round of golf.

"We want to give you the honor of teeing off first." Greg said to Matt as they stretched their muscles at the first tee box.

"I wanted to earn the honor of teeing off first, but I don't think I will earn that honor anytime soon." Matt responded as he pulled out his driver.

"It really doesn't matter who has the honor." Clark chimed in. "We're just glad you enjoy playing with us old farts. Ever since Kindall

died, we've been missing our threesome."

"Sounds good to me," Matt answered as he placed his ball on the tee. "He took a couple practice swings, then looked down the fairway. He started to approach his ball but stopped and raised his leg up, bending

his knee.

"Not done stretching?" Greg asked.

"No." Matt answered. Just a little tingle in my knee.

"I'm probably a little nervous about starting off the round for the first time."

They all laughed, and he refocused on making the shot. He looked down the fairway, paused for a moment, then approached the ball. He stepped up, took a swing, and struck the ball straight down the fairway.

"Wow, what a shot!" Greg yelled. "Good Lord!" Clark added.

"You just drove that ball about three hundred yards straight down the fairway. I've only seen you drive the ball about two hundred yards all the times we have played!"

"Must be adrenalin." Matt explained.

"Probably the excitement of taking the first shot."

"Whatever it is," Greg added, "looks like you're ready to play today."

At the end of the round, the threesome were in the parking lot taking off their golf shoes.

"You played golf today," Clark said to Matt, as he shook his hand. "You beat us for the first time. It was only a matter of time before you

young whippersnapper caught up and passed us oldsters." "I didn't think it would happen." Matt answered.

"Especially this fast. Y'all are experienced golfers, and play on a regular basis."

"I'll have nightmares tonight about the putts I missed," Greg joked. "Just like my daughter."

"Your daughter has nightmares?" Matt asked in a serious tone. "Yeah. She wakes up in the night with dreams about dead people.

Sometimes they are people who Samatha knew who has passed on."

"Let me ask you something," Matt said as he finished tying his street shoes. "Does Samatha drink a lot of sodas or fruit juices, and eat a lot of sweets?"

"Yeah. Probably more than she should, like a lot of kids do."

"Well," Matt responded. "Without getting so technical and acting like I'm a doctor, the brain produces our dreams. Like the rest of the body, the brain needs good nourishment to work at its best. The brain fluid that surrounds and cushions the brain from the skull is full of the nourishing ingredients to feed the brain."

"Sodas, and even fruit juices, contain caffeine, artificial coloring, sucrose, traces of lead, and mercury."

"They have supposedly taken brominated vegetable oil, or BVD from sodas, but I wouldn't trust it. BVD was patented as a flame retardant, and was studied to cause neurological conditions in mice."

"Those chemicals affect the brain function, and limit the positive effects of healthy foods and beverages."

"Try giving her water and whole milk. More water will take more needed oxygen to the brain. Milk will provide protein, calcium, vitamin D, riboflavin, and potassium to the brain. This will nourish the brain and help it function better, which should limit bad dreams."

"I'll give it a try." Greg said.

"While you're at it, doctor," Clark intervened, "what can I do about this ringing in my ears?"

"Not much." Matt answered.

"That ringing is actually the sound of your brain working. You actually hear the firing of the electric signals of your brain working."

"Well, I'll be damned!" Clark exclaimed. "So, I can literally hear myself think?"

"Yes," Matt answered. "It may be comforting to know your brain is doing what it is supposed to do."

"See you guys next week."

Meanwhile, at the Karate studio, Tangie tangled with her sparring partner. She flipped him over her back and slammed him hard on the floor. He squirmed and grimaced with the hard slam.

"I'm sorry." she said to him, surprised by the unexpectedly aggressive move.

Her instructor walked up to them, and she helped her partner to his feet. "Pretty solid move." the instructor reacted.

"I didn't teach you that move. Since you are so advanced in your training, I want to enter you in a regional tournament next month."

• • •

That evening at home, the couple reflected on their day.

"I shot a seventy-five today!" Matt said excitedly. "It was my first time shooting in the seventies."

"Congratulations! I knew you would figure it out." she answered. "It was just a matter of staying positive and being patient."

"It felt like it was more than that," he returned.

"Before my swing, it was like my mind just told me to go straight back and take a straight swing, like the testing machine they use to test golf balls. My mind said forget all of the lessons and types of swings I have tried and just swing like the machine. And the ball went straight and far."

"It finally clicked for you," she said.

"Well, we'll see if it continues or if I revert to old form. Golf can't be as simple as it was today."

"Also, I felt a tingle in my knee right before I started playing today. It was where I hurt my knee from falling off that horse. I wondered if I would have any effects from that injury as I got older. Looks like it's starting to happen, but it didn't affect my game. I just hope it doesn't hurt my ability to get around on the course as I get older."

"I have faith in you. You are in good physical condition, and will be able to play a long time." she said, as she planted a light kiss on his lips.

"My day was surprisingly different. I put a move on my sparring partner I never performed before. I almost injured him, but he was okay. My

instructor has me sparring with men because no women were at my level."
"It's like I could see the next move clearly in my mind, and I just followed what I saw. I felt like I wanted to be aggressive today. Not sure what came over me."

"The instructor wants me to enter tournaments. I'm not sure about that. I just want to stay in shape, know how to defend myself, and teach you what I know."

"I'm willing to learn." Matt responded. "I want you to teach me all you know. I don't want to have to have you protect me."

"You bet!" she responded. "I'll teach you to be better than I am. That's possible because you're physically stronger than I am."

"And that's what I'm concentrating about, protection. I'm not interested in competing against people who are trained to compete in the ring. I'm interested in learning to compete against the street fighters, those who don't play by any rules. Those who will do anything to hurt you, make any move against you. Those who really want to hurt you. That's what my training is all about."

"I think what I felt today when the man came out on the floor was a deep instinct to protect myself and be aggressive. Make any move I had in me. It was like fight or flight instincts of our brains. I knew I wasn't going to leave. I was going to use what I knew."

"And that's what I want to learn from you, baby," he responded. "Like you, I want to learn the protective and counter moves to use against the unconventional attackers of the world. Why don't we start with my first formal training lesson right now."

"Right here?" she asked. "Right now?"

"Here and now. Actually, let's go to the den and take off our shoes."
"Okay, let's do it."

They walked to the den, removed their shoes, and started performing stretching routines.

"I want you to teach me everything that you know," he said as he finished stretching, and faced her.

"Okay." she responded. "Let's start with a simple, quick, but effective defensive technique for getting away from someone's grasp."

"Most people grab and hold people from behind, and most of the time it is a male. I want you to come behind me and grasp me holding my arms down." Matt did as instructed.

"You know how sensitive the groin area of a male is?" she asked. "I do."

"People hold people with their legs apart for more balance." she said. "And the smarter ones will hold their head to one side to keep you from head butting them in the face with the back of your head. That slightly side hold puts them in the perfect position that leaves the groin area open and vulnerable for attack. All you have to do is kick backward to the groin like this." She kicked her leg backwards between his legs.

"Even if your heel doesn't reach the groin the first time, keep kicking. Most of the time, their natural reaction is to protect that area. They will either loosen their grip on you, or try to protect that area with one hand and try to hold you with the other. This gives you the opportunity to escape. If they tighten their grip to try to keep you from kicking, they will usually twist and turn you away from kicking that area. This can make them lose balance. When they sway one way, sway with them. This will cause a fall. They will usually use one hand to cushion their fall, again giving you the chance to get away. If they hold on tight, you now have leverage to roll them using your legs. But you have to do it quickly, because they will be trying to clamp your legs with their legs."

"When you kick them in the groin with your heel and they let go, they will almost always grab that area. You can run, but if you decide to counterattack, they will be bent over. They will be in a perfect position for an uppercut to the chin or eyes, or a roundhouse punch to the temple." "A hard hit to the chin can break their jawbone. A punch to the eyes can put an eye out. Also, a chin hit may cause them to bite their tongue pretty severely, because they may either be yelling at you or screaming in

pain from the groin hit."

Tangie then turned around, faced Matt, and wrapped her arms around him.

"If someone grabs you from the front, they will still usually open their legs for balance. This again gives the opportunity to go for the groin kicking your knee forward, like this." She demonstrated a forward knee kick.

"I don't advise using a head butt." she said. "That only works in the movies where only the one doing the head butting doesn't also get injured. You have to execute it perfectly to keep from getting hurt yourself."

"If their face is squarely in front of yours, look down at their mouth and bang your head quickly against theirs, looking at their mouth. This will bring the hardest part of your face, your forehead, into their nose, giving you the opportunity to break their nose. If they believe their nose is broken, they will let at least one of their arms go and tend to their nose, again giving you the opportunity to get away. But only take the nose shot if they are still and you believe you have a good shot at their nose."

"Have you got this?"

"I do," he answered. "Now let me go through it." He then did everything she demonstrated.

"You're doing great," she said, after he was done. "This is a good start." Then she changed the subject.

"Hey, are you ready to go to church with me tomorrow?" she asked, with an air of hopefulness.

"Believe me, I'm getting close."

"Mainly because you are so connected, and I really want to understand Christianity. And I love you, and want us to share as much as we can."

"I want to spend some time tomorrow learning and working on your car's electric engine. You know I like to understand how things work, especially things I own."

"You drive the Mercedes to church. How about another self-defense lesson?"

"Okay. Let's go to the next technique. We'll continue working on defensive moves before we go to offensive moves. Just promise me you will teach me to shoot as well as I teach you how to fight."

"I promise."

Later that evening, Matt sat on his sofa relaxing and started reading a book. Tangie approached him, handing him a bottled water.

"What are you reading?"

"I picked up some books that may help us learn a little more about meditation, ESP, relaxation, and electromagnetic brain activity."

She saw one book in his hand, and three others on the coffee table beside the sofa. She read the titles of each one of the books.

"*The Ancient Art of Hindu Meditation*," she called out as she pulled the first book from his hands. Then she picked up the second book and read its title, "*ESP And Mental Telepathy Are Real Phenomena*." Then she picked up the third book.

"*Far East and South Asian Mental Art.*" Then she read the fourth book's title, "*Electrical Impulses and Power of the Brain.*"

"I think these books can help us obtain more brain clarity and do our jobs a little better." he said, defending the literature.

"I don't know." she responded.

"You know they want us to draw on our own abilities without any outside influences. These books may be considered outside influences. The same as if we had come from working another job that had taught us different techniques."

"I may not go that route." "Suit yourself," he responded.

"I look at it as continuing education."

"But is it continuing education they would approve?"

"I can ask them." he answered. "I know they want our minds to be free of any outside interference or influence, but I think they also want us to be able to improvise intellectually, otherwise they would just bring in any smart people and teach them their ways. I believe they want us to get to a desirable outcome by using our brains to implement processes of our own to get the desired results."

"I see what you're saying." she responded. "They may be okay if an outside process or idea is introduced. But I think it may be okay only if the outside information acquired sparks something in us to use and develop into something we can use to go to another level of knowledge and performance unrelated to that outside influence."

"That sounds technically correct." Matt responded. "And that's what I believe I am doing."

15

MONDAY EXERCISE

The two arrived at their Level 2 lab anticipating the next task for them. "Good morning. Time for your next exercise." the voice said, after the couple entered the lab and sat at a table that had two pens and two writing pads on it.

One of the small compartment doors slid open, and out slid a tray with two metal bands that looked like headbands.

"These are polygraph bands. They are more accurate in measuring physical and emotional reactions than your standard lie detector used by regular law enforcement agencies. They will beep when you lie. A light on the band will light up red when you tell the truth."

"There are yes or no questions. They will be simple questions. You will nod or shake your head, and write yes or no on the pads on the table." "Strap the bands around your head. It will take five seconds for the bands to read your vital signs and brain processes."

They strapped on the bands. Lights on the bands started blinking. After five seconds, their first names appeared on a wall screen. Their vital signs came up line by line under their names.

The voice started again.

"Your job is to deliberately lie to the questions asked and pass the polygraph. In other words, the lie detector will say you passed the test, but you actually answered the questions incorrectly."

"Matt, I will start with you." "Does two plus two equals five?"

Matt paused a few seconds, then nodded his head, and wrote down "yes."

The light on his band blinked red.

"Well done." the voice said. "Now your turn Tangie." "Two plus two equals five?"

Tangie paused a few seconds, then nodded her head, and wrote down "yes."

The band beeped, indicating she was not telling the truth. "Matt." The voice went back to him.

"Does April come on the calendar before January?" Matt nodded his head, and wrote down "yes." Again, the light on his band blinked red.

The voice asked the question to Tangie, and she failed the test again.

This exercise continued for the remainder of the day with different false questions and the same results from the couple.

"You passed a lie detector test by lying!" Tangie said in amazement, as the couple drove home.

"I think I was just calm," Matt responded. "I think it was because I always believed you could lie and pass a polygraph test."

"You're obviously on a faster track than I am to zeroing in and controlling your brain functions, emotions, and physical reactions," she said proudly.

"I have a ways to go. And it seems we have a ways to go before we are producing actual value to our job goals."

The exercise continued all week with the same results.

"Tonight, I will pray for favor and greater success on my job," Tangie said on their way home that Friday evening.

Monday morning, Tangie strapped the polygraph band around her head with optimistic anticipation.

The voice addressed her with a question.

"Tangie, the Earth has more than one moon."

Tangie answered yes. The red light came on. She smiled.

They both answered the questions incorrectly and passed the poly- graph the remainder of the week.

That Friday night, they reflect on the week and upcoming weekend. "We had our best week ever!" Matt exclaimed. "Let's celebrate by

having Chinese tonight!" "Okay, sounds good!"

"It's amazing what the mind can do. I am starting to feel we are just scratching the surface of what the brain can do."

"Do you think they will have another exercise for us Monday?"

"Not sure. But they hired us to be productive, and we need to start producing at some point."

"My golfing buddy Clark mentioned that he has ringing in the ear.

I'm starting to think about how to cure that problem."

"Well," she chimed in. "You know those billions of neurons that carry information from the brain to the rest of the body communicate in the form of electrical pulses at the synapses. Those firing points are not exactly totally quiet."

"Too bad the ear canal is so close to those firing points, and that sound comes through to many people."

"Well," he came back, "that issue is going to take some work on our part, but I believe we can do something about it."

"Yes," she agreed.

"Changing the subject, how about you attend church with me Sunday?" "Okay, okay."

"Great!" she responded, and leaned over and gave him a kiss.

• • •

Saturday morning, Matt met with his golfing buddies Clark and Greg. Greg approached as Matt exited his car.

"Your suggestion worked!" Greg shouted excitedly, and he reached to shake Matt's hand.

"Since you said we should give Samatha only milk and water to drink, and cut down on her sweets, her nightmares have gone away."

"That's great!" Matt answered, and he reached out and shook Greg's hand.

"Why don't more people know this simple method of controlling bad dreams?" Greg asked.

"I don't think there's been a study on it." Matt answered.

"And I'm not sure how many people would follow that kind of diet." "I can see that." Greg returned.

"Samatha will want to drink her other drinks, and eat some sweets. But at least we know the cause, and can control it. I'm so glad you told me that. Now she has a chance to have a happy life free of nagging nightmares."

CHAPTER

16

SUNDAY SERMON

"The title of my teaching today is, 'Stop Blaming God,'" the pastor said, after the choir exited the stage.

"Most non-Christians, and even many Christians, blame God for the work of the devil. And many nonbelievers say the Bible contradicts itself."

"Our God is a God of love, and we live under new covenant of the New Testament, started by Jesus Christ, who died for our sins. And we are covered by the blood of Jesus, and are in good standing with God when we accept Jesus as our Lord and Savior."

"We do not live under Old Testament laws. However, even many Christians still live by Old Testament beliefs, such as that God punishes us for things we do, or certain laws such as not eating certain food, not doing certain things on Sunday, and many other traditions of the Old Testament." "Adam was influenced by the devil, and brought sin into the world.

The devil is the author of sin, and the world is cursed with sin."

"John Ten, Ten says the devil comes only to steal and kill and destroy.

Jesus says I have come that you may have life, and have it abundantly."

"The devil comes in many forms."

Hebrews chapter ten tells us that the old laws were a shadow of things to come. That man could not do enough to atone and stay atoned for sin. That the sacrifice of animals does not permanently take away sins. Jesus came as that one sacrifice for all mankind."

"Hebrews chapter eight, verses six and seven says, 'He has obtained a more excellent ministry inasmuch as He is also Mediator of a better covenant, which was established on better promises. For if that first covenant had been faultless, then no place would have been sought for a second.'"

"In this new covenant, we can look at verses like John Ten Ten, where Jesus wants us to have a good life."

"Third John One Two says, 'Beloved, I pray that you may prosper in all things, and be in good health, just as your soul prospers.'"

"John Two Fourteen says, 'Glory to God in the highest, and on earth peace, goodwill toward men.'"

"This means that God has declared peace with man when Jesus was born."

"God promised us one hundred and twenty years, and He wants us to live every bit of it."

"The devil is doing his work to destroy you and make you blame God. Some people even hate God because they blame Him for the work of the devil."

"We say things like, 'God took them. It was their time. God called them home.'"

"God is punishing me or you for something. God did this to get your attention."

"God sent that storm because the people were evil." "Why would God do this?"

"Why did God let them die?"

"Many Bible-toting, scripture-quoting people say and believe these things."

"There are reasons people experience the negative issues of this world." "As I said, this world is cursed. Adam made sure of that."

"Storms, tornadoes, and famines are results of a fallen world. Jesus himself warned of earthquakes and wars."

"Wicked and ignorant living certainly contributes to early death. We violate our bodies with drugs, illicit sex, unhealthy eating, not keeping in good physical condition."

"And certainly not having faith and not accepting Jesus blocks out the good things God wants for you."

"I believe this message was meant for someone today."

"Well Tangie," Matt started the conversation reflection on the sermon on their drive home.

"The pastor's sermon actually made sense to me. I'm not where you are, but my door is open to your Christian world. There are still a lot of questions in my mind."

"I have always been positive about you, and have been praying for you," she said with a smile.

"I know the logical side of your brain that doesn't compute the unseen. You have a hard time accepting what you feel is not scientifically proven. But I am glad you have started that move. There's more in this world than math and science."

"But it's all about love. And I have faith in you because I believe you know about love."

"I look at it as a journey. You have left the station, and are on the right train."

Matt responded, "He said many things that made me think. He has me rethinking my mother's death. And he said the devil comes in many forms. That's when the injured scar on my knee tingled."

CHAPTER

17

NEXT PHASE OF LEVEL 2

On Monday morning, the couple walked into the Level 2 lab. They were surprised to see the room had a partition in the middle. The voice came on.

"Welcome Matt and Tangie to the next phase of your job. You have men- tally prepared yourselves for this part of the training. Now it's time to put you to task, as well as increase your level of concentration, and test your resolve." "For the rest of your time in Level Two, you will work separately on separate tasks. You are NOT, I repeat NOT, to discuss with each other what you are doing. You have followed this order thus far with everyone

else in your lives. Now you will expand that capability with each other." "You will be given different tasks over the screen or in ear buds. You will not be asked to do the same task at the same time the other is per- forming that task."

For the next six weeks, the couple perform various tasks, including breaking world memory records, memorizing short books and reciting them from back to front, predicting the next section of various sequences of questions and programs, and animal and people movements.

Then they came to the seventh week.

"Now," the voice says to them, "your next assignment will be to go to your respective rooms and mentally give each other assignments."

"You will only telepath assignments the other can perform in the room, with and only with the things they can retrieve by pushing a button for such things as cards and programs."

"When you believe you have received your assignment from the other, you will perform it. You will compare notes at the end of the day, and record your findings."

They performed this exercise for three weeks with varying degrees of success.

CHAPTER

18

A VISIT TO THE ORPHANAGE

Flo ran to the car with a big smile to meet Matt and Tangie as they parked in the lot of her orphanage.

"It's so great to see you two again!" she called loudly, as she approached the car to hug both of them. "Your financial donation is great, but it's even better to see y'all again in person."

"It's so good to see you again!" they both said as they hugged her back.

"I can't wait to show y'all around," Flo said as they walked to the main building.

"I know y'all can't tell me about your work, but you can say how things are going."

"Things are moving along," Matt said, as they walked into the building. "And Matt is attending church now." Tangie said with a glow. "Hallelujah!" Flo stopped and yelled. "God is good!"

"And things are going well here. We have kids from age two to twenty-two."

"It's unfortunate that for many of these children their parents did not want them. Some are runaways. The paperwork on some of them is very difficult to gather or create, but it's worth it to help them transition to a more stable environment."

"We show a lot of love because we operate on God and good Christian values in a good Christian environment."

"We have an adoption record here better than the national average."
"Let's go this way to the Day Room."

They walked into a large room. Children were in the room playing with various games.

"Hey everyone." Flo called. "Say hello to Matt and Tangie Riley."
"Hello Mister and Misses Riley!" the kids respectfully greeted the couple. Some waved to them with their vocal greeting. "Hello everyone!" Tangie called.

"Hi kids!" Matt followed. "We're happy to see you all for the first time, but you will see more of us in the future."

Flo started walking through the room, and they followed her.

"See y'all later." Tangie called as they walked toward the end of the room.

"Bye bye." The kids responded.

As they approached the hallway at the end of the room, they noticed a seven-year-old boy sitting alone. Flo noticed that they noticed him.

"That's Jamie," Flo said, anticipating that they would ask about him. "He has been here about a year now."

"He's very quiet. Doesn't say much, and doesn't interact much. We don't try to force him to do or say anything. I believe he will come around. He must have had a very traumatic experience."

"Mental Health Services brought him here and asked if we would care for him. They said the police found him wandering out of the woods. They had no papers on him, so I just call him Jamie until we find out more about him."

"I read a scripture and pray with him in my arms every day." Tangie and Matt walked over to him.

"Hi Jamie." They both called, and smiled at him.

He looked up at them, but did not say anything. They walked back to Flo.

"We felt the need to speak to him," Tangie said as they started walking out of the room.

The two looked back at Jamie as they left the room. He was still looking at them.

The three walked outside.

"Look at the gardens," Flo said as she pointed to the vegetable garden. "We produce food for the market here. It is good work for the children." "Let's go see the kids working with the animals," she said as they

walked past the tomatoes and corn in the fields.

"We have some dogs, horses, and goats," she said, as they approached the horse stalls. "They love working with the animals. They ride the horses. The dogs love the kids. And you won't believe how much the kids love goats."

"Goats are very intelligent. More intelligent than most people realize. They make excellent pets. They are my favorite animal to work with. They are always looking like they can understand what you are thinking. That's something you two can relate to."

"For sure." Matt responded. "And I enjoyed horses growing up. The scar on my knee reminds me of that. Don't think that one horse agreed with me."

"After the animals, I want to go to our chapel," Flo said, as they walked through the horse pen.

At the end of the tour, Flo walked the couple to their car.

"It's so great to see y'all again. Don't be a stranger. You are welcome here anytime," Flo said, as she gave them a goodbye hug.

"We'll be back real soon," Tangie said, as she returned the hug.

As they drove off, Tangie offered her opinion of their encounter with one of the orphans.

"I feel like Jamie wanted to say something to us," she said.

"I think we will understand what he is trying to say as we spend more time there," Matt said in a confident tone.

"Now let me turn on some seventies music."

They turned off I-25 onto a two-lane shortcut road heading back to Carlsbad.

They drove for about twenty minutes. Then Matt spoke.

"I feel that tingle in my knee," he said as he reached down to rub his knee.

"You have done a lot of driving and walking today," Tangie responded. "Does it hurt?"

"No. It's just a bit of a tingle. Maybe the walking at the orphanage does have something to do with it. Plus seeing those horses brought back memories."

"I'll pull over and rub it a bit to see if it goes away. Maybe I better slow down on those martial arts lessons you are giving me. You are an expert, and you move pretty fast."

A few seconds after they pulled off the road, a car came speeding up toward them. It was swerving a bit on both sides of the road. They looked up and saw the car approaching, as they could hear the tires screeching.

It passed by them on the wrong side of the road. They watched in shock as the lone driver kept on driving at a high rate of speed, well over the speed limit.

"He's driving on the wrong side of the road!" Tangie hollered.

"He must be drugged or drunk," Matt added. "I'll call the police and report him. I hope they catch him before he hurts or kills himself or someone else."

"He could have hurt or killed us if we hadn't pulled over," she said with her eyes wide open and covering her mouth with one hand. "Thank God for His protection."

They arrived home.

"I suppose I should start leading our Bible reading, since I'm the man of the house," he said as they walked through the door.

"That would be super!" she responded with excitement.

"For some reason I have Psalm Ninety One in my mind. I remember your pastor using that one when he dismisses us."

"That's a Psalm declaring angelic protection over us," she said. "That's what happened to us on the road today. That's no coincidence.

I believe God is working with you." "I don't know about that."

"I'm still evaluating this Christian thing. I don't think He would use me. I'm skeptical, and have no experience. I just started reading the Bible, and that's mainly because of you."

"It doesn't matter what your level of experience or commitment is," she responded.

"Jesus chose Paul to spread the gospel of Christianity to the world.

Before Paul converted, he persecuted Christians."

"All of the people in the Bible had flaws, except Jesus. If God only chose perfect people to use, He would not have anyone to work with."

"Jonah tried to run from God's command."

"Elijah wanted to abandon his mission. I can go on and on about the issues great men of God had at some point in their lives. You're with me for a reason."

"I don't know about all that," he responded. "Don't put me further down the line than I am." "It's not me."

"Since we're talking about unknown feelings," he said. "I'm having some thoughts about the piece of metal Flo gave us."

"What more can we do with it?" she responded. "We've had it analyzed, and they did not come up with the metallic makeup."

"But it is some type of metal. And I believe it's our mission to find out how it can be used."

The next day, the couple came home from church. Matt picked up the metal object.

"I'm attracted to this thing," he said, as he tossed it into the air a couple times. "But now I'm going out to work on the EV." He put the object in his pocket.

As he stepped into the garage, he felt a bit of an electrical pulse from the object in his pocket. He stopped and pulled it out of his pocket. He examined it, and it seemed to vibrate a bit. He ran back into the house.

"I felt something from this thing!" he said, as he approached Tangie. "What?" she asked.

"It kind of vibrated and felt a little warm when I went to the garage." "But it doesn't feel like that now."

"Go with me to the garage, and let's see if it happens again." They walked to the garage. He handed the object to her.

"I think I feel it!" she said as they walk into the garage. "What do you think is going on?"

"I don't know, but I think it has something to do with something out here in the garage. I told you there's something strange about this thing. Flo knew it."

"I believe it's some unworldly object that gets an electrical charge when it gets near something," she said.

19

NEXT LEVEL 2 TASK

The couple walked into their lab, and was greeted by the familiar voice. "Good morning, Matt and Tangie."

"Today we start a new task."

"Please walk to the large doors on your respective sides."

Tangie's door slid opened. Behind a cage was a male chimpanzee. The chimp jumped toward the front of the cage. Tangie jumped back. Matt's door opened. A male goat stood in a cage.

"Your task," the voice stated. "is to communicate with your animals, of course without talking."

"You will progress with them to the point of giving them orders such as speaking, sitting, walking, and nodding affirmative or negative."

"You will continue your daily routine of summarizing your tasks and progress or lack of progress on a daily basis."

Tangie walked up to the cage and bent down and smiled at the primate. The chimp looked up at her. The ape looked her right in the eyes for several minutes. She smiled at him. She felt that she was immediately developing a relationship with him.

She stood up and walked to the left side of the cage. The chimp hopped over to her side, and continued to stare up at her. She knelt down again and smiled. He curved his lips as if he was attempting to smile back at her. She held out her hand as if attempting to offer a handshake. He looked down at her arm, then put both of his hands behind his head. She felt he was offering a sarcastic and humorous gesture in deference to her move.

She laughed and put her hands to her face after seeing the chimp make his move.

The chimp then put his hands to his face and made a slight bellow as if mocking and laughing at her. She laughed even more after his laughing sound.

Meanwhile, Matt walked over to the goat cage. The goat moved his mouth in a chewing motion, as though he had just been fed.

Matt knelt down and leaned on the cage, looking at the goat. The goat continued his chewing motioned, and looked around as if expecting to receive more food.

Matt tried to get the goat's attention by walking from side to side of the cage and waving his hands. But the goat appeared disinterested, and continued looking as though he wanted to continue eating. Matt believed the goat was fed, as he correctly assumed the animals would not be presented to them if they were not adequately fed. Otherwise, the animals would only be concentrating on getting food, and would probably only pay attention to their trainers with the goal of being fed on their minds.

The next week, both Tangie and Matt had given their animals names in their notes. Tangie named her chimp friend Gabby, as she related the noises the animal was making to his trying to talk to her. Matt named his goat Poker, from the animal's poker face look no matter what Matt did to get the goat's attention.

After seven weeks of working with the animals, Matt and Tangie were getting just about the same results as the first week when they were introduced to the animals. The chimp imitated all of Tangie's moves. The goat still appeared indifferent to anything Matt did. Neither trainer received any response from the animals when they just looked at the animals and tried to communicate telepathically.

Both Matt and Tangie studied and concentrated on the transmission of neurons for both their brains and the brains of their subjects. Matt started using the deep breathing and mind clearing techniques of Buddhist monks.

He wanted to recommend those techniques to Tangie, but knew that would break their instructions of not sharing anything about their jobs to each other.

CHAPTER

20

BREAKTHROUGH

By the ninth week of working with the animals, Tangie and Gabby were having fun imitating each other. Gabby had learned what Tangie's next move would be before she would do it. She had a routine of making certain moves, then changing up the moves.

Gabby had developed a sense of what her next move would be before she made the gesture. He did not follow any instructions when Tangie tried to communicate with him telepathically. Instead, he would gesture that he wanted to continue playing the follow-the-leader games. When Tangie wanted to take a break, Gabby would motion for her to continue playing with him.

Tangie decided to change the routine. She decided to put Gabby in a position to make the first move or come up with the first thought. She sat down and just looked at the chimp. She could see in his eyes that he was expecting her to make a move. She just looked at him in a somber manner. Gabby lost his usual anticipatory and excited disposition. He started to look at her in a concerned manner.

She looked away from him for a few minutes. She could feel his concern. She turned back around and looked at him with a sad look. She could feel the chimpanzee ask her, *"Is there a problem with you today?"* She documented her findings.

A similar story developed with Matt and Poker. Matt had decided to bring two magnets with him. He thought the magnetic fields of the magnets may have some interaction and effect with the natural magnetic fields of the human and animal brain.

He also started to use the techniques he had learned from the meditation and telepathy books he had purchased and discussed with Tangie. Matt sat down on the floor, crossed his legs, and started deep breathing techniques. He also developed a picture of the human brain in his mind, as well as a goat brain.

He noticed Poker started sitting when he would sit. When he started closing his eyes, he would peek out one eye and notice Poker had started closing his eyes.

Matt held the two magnets up over his ears on each side of his head.

Poker immediately came over and looked into Matt's eyes.

Matt called out Poker's name in his mind as he looked at the animal.

Poker immediately looked up at Matt.

The look on Poker's face and eyes made Matt feel like the animal was saying to him, *"I heard you, Matt. What do you want to say?"*

Matt looked at him and commanded in his mind, *"Go to the back corner on my left and lie down."* The goat did as commanded.

Then Matt telepathically commanded, *"Come back here and speak to me."* The goat got up, walked to Matt, and let out a loud bellow.

Matt said, *"Thank you,"* from his mind to the goat. Poker shook his head with an up and down affirmative motion.

Matt wondered if he could successfully make a command to Poker without the goat looking at him. He knew that in order for the program to be successful, people would need to be able to telepathically send commands without the other person's knowledge or presence.

When Poker looked away, Matt relaxed and tried to focus his brain-waves onto Poker. He commanded Poker to stand up and walk to him. Poker turned and looked at Matt. Then Poker stood up and walked to him at the front of the cage.

Matt's eyes lit up as he rushed over to record his notes of what he felt was a breakthrough with his telepathic communication.

As usual, he recorded the information on an internal secure system.

But he also backed up the data on a removable chip drive.

By the end of the week, Porker followed all of Matt's telepathic commands. This revelation made Matt start wondering if he would be successful on humans.

On Friday evening, at the end of the very successful week, Matt and Tangie relaxed in their living room.

Matt watched television. Tangie picked up one of Matt's books on Buddha meditation, and started to read it.

It was late in the evening approaching bed time when Matt started thinking about sending a telepathic command to Tangie. He slumped down and pretended to be dozing off. He started his meditation and self-hypnosis. He pictured the command center of his brain while he peeped at his wife.

He locked in on the receptive and motion functions of her brain. He commanded her to go get him something to drink from the refrigerator.

Tangie put down her book, stood up, and walked to the fridge. He peeked at her walking to the kitchen.

While Matt was in his self-induced hypnotic state, he experienced a memory flashback. His mind reverted back to the night he and Tangie were abducted.

A quick flash of him looking in his rearview mirror and seeing the lights approaching the car ran through his mind.

The memory flash quickly woke Matt up from his trance. He sat up and looked around, assuring himself that he was safe in his home.

"I thought you could use this," Tangie said, as she handed Matt a bottled water.

"Thank you," Matt said as he sat back and reflected on his flashback.

He did not mention his experience to Tangie, as he tried to process in his mind what had just happened. He thought about that night the rest of the evening.

CHAPTER

21

ALIEN CONVERSION

Back aboard the craft that abducted Matt and Tangie, the aliens discussed the chip they implanted into Matt.

"The chip is not working as we planned," the first alien telepathically communicated to the group of five other aliens.

"What is it not doing for us?" another alien asked.

"It is not providing information on what the human is doing. And it is not reading his brain thoughts and knowledge," the first alien answered.

"Then what is it doing as we programmed it?" a third alien asked. "It is providing his location," the first alien answered.

"We can track his movement. But it appears there is some type of interference that is blocking us from sending and receiving any other information to and from him."

"He may be picking up another signal that is stronger than ours right now." "So, this chip is not doing us much good?" a fourth alien asked. "Not under the present circumstances," the first alien answered. "The chip we have developed since we abducted that couple should work much better."

"So, we need to re-abduct the human, remove that chip from his knee, and replace it with the newer one," the fifth alien commanded.

"Since we are able to keep up with his whereabouts, we just wait for the right time and place to bring him back."

"We need this same human, instead of going with another mortal right now. This one has the intellect and brain structure that we need to work with to accomplish our goals."

"He is super intelligent. He doesn't believe in God. He is working on secret projects. And he will be fathering children, children who will carry on our works."

"We have been studying him too long to start over with somebody new. From monitoring his life history, we know that he doesn't believe in UFO's. That means the probability that he will undergo hypnosis is extremely remote. If he doesn't take the intelligence quotient tests, it is very unlikely that he will subject himself to a hypnotist. We know hypnosis helps many humans recall and re-live their abduction experiences."

"And to add to the perfection of this project with him, the scar on his knee was the perfect place to hide the chip. We didn't need to make a mark that he or someone else could become suspicious about."

"His very pattern of behavior, beliefs, and physical makeup makes him the perfect human to work with and to work through."

"You know, we looked at a couple Black Americans who have tremendous potential because when they are positioned in the right environments they are very creative. But their deep Christian roots make it harder to work with them. And the pervasive systemic racism in society limits their opportunities to be placed in the areas where we need them to be."

"We don't have a presence in that facility where this Matt Riley human works. We have to find out what is going on in there."

"We know how the American government likes to hide its projects from its people. People eventually found out a lot about Area Fifty One and Area Fifty Two."

"We have our spies in Los Alamos and other facilities. But it appears neither the American people, nor our spies, know anything about the New Mexico facility."

"We have got to abduct him again. This time we will plant the new chip in both of them."

22

LEVEL 5 MEETING

The G.O.D facility Level 5 participants discussed the Rileys.

The room was a smallish rectangular shape. It had screens on each of the longer walls facing each other. The room did not have any windows.

There was a board meeting table in the middle of the room. No one sat in the chairs at the table.

The screens turned on.

On the first screen, an American man appeared. On the second screen popped up a Columbian official.

"Good morning, Mr. Fernando." the American spoke.

"Good morning, Mr. Dunn," Mr. Fernando returned the greeting. "I am happy to announce great news," Mr. Dunn continued.

"It appears we are at a breakthrough point of our project. Our employees seem to have cracked the code for mind control, providing a tremendous opportunity for us to achieve our goals. We should be ready for human trials very soon."

"This is great news!" Mr. Fernando exclaimed. Mr. Dunn continued.

"We will soon have the secret weapon the United States and Columbia need to control our population's need and dependency on illegal drugs. This will make America truly great. We will not lose so many good people to drug abuse. And the good part about it is that we can get them off drugs without using drugs."

"This is a secret weapon that will remain a secret weapon known only by our governments," Mr. Dunn chimed back in.

"Both countries will benefit greatly. America will have thirty percent more productivity. In turn, Columbia will become a much safer country to visit. And any lost money on the drug trade and police corruption will be made up with American tourism that our governments will be promoting." "Columbia will be the new vacation capital of the world!" Mr. Fernando exclaimed.

"We will use mind control to get Americans off drugs, and to vacation Columbia. We will be a safe and rich country, and surpass Europe and other places Americans love to go."

"We will build a great infrastructure and tourist attractions second to none!"

"And we will become a more powerful country that China and Russia cannot touch," Mr. Dunn replied. "Then the CIA can do what they want to with Level Four."

Then he concluded the meeting.

"That's all I have for now. I will call another meeting in the very near future."

The screens went blank.

As soon as his screen went off, Mr. Dunn picked up his secured private phone and made a call to Moscow, Russia. A Russian official answered his phone in his office near the Kremlin.

"Comrade Dunn, I have been waiting for you to call me," the man said with a smile in his Russian accent.

"Mr. Volenski," Mr. Dunn responded.

"How are you? Are you freezing your butt off in Moscow." "It's not that cold," Mr. Volenski answered.

"You'll be surprised what a little Russian vodka does for the body." "But I need some news from you that could be even warmer. How are

your American Einsteins progressing?"

"That's what I wanted to report."

"Seems our American Einsteins are living up to their billing. We believe they have cracked the code to human telepathy and mind control."

"That's wonderful news," Mr. Volenski responded.

"So, we will soon have the key to controlling American behavior and actions. By controlling their behavior, we can make them do anything we want, including destroying all of their nuclear weapons."

"This will fulfill Nikita Khrushchev's prediction back in the nineteen fifties that Russia will take over America without firing a shot."

"This will also make you a very rich man, Mr. Dunn. And if you deliver the contents of Level Four, we will be the most technologically advanced country in the world. There won't even be a close second."

"I'll drink a vodka to that," Mr. Dunn said as he lifted a bottled water up in the air.

"And thanks for this secret phone. My employer, the CIA, listens to everything on other wave bands."

At the same time, Mr. Fernando signed off the meeting and turned around to a fellow Columbian official in the room.

"Looks like those two American geniuses have learned how to control human behavior without drugs," Mr. Fernando said to the other official.

"This is very good news for us," the other official answered.

"This is a very ironic state of affairs for our country. We can make America even more drug dependent without using drugs to make them want even more drugs."

"We will soon be able to saturate America with our drugs. This will make us the richest country in the world. And we will be able to control the United States."

"Yes!" Mr. Fernando agreed.

"We need to send in a team to kidnap the couple before the Americans start using this information."

"And I need to call a meeting with Mr. Dunn."

23

SOME TIME OFF WORK

"It's great to have some time off for the holiday season," Tangie said, with a smile as she poured Matt some milk into a glass at their kitchen table. It was the Monday of Thanksgiving week. They would be off work the whole week. "Yes, it is," Matt agreed.

"We're off this week and then three weeks for Christmas. I can use some time off to relax."

"Speaking of relaxing," Tangie returned, "you were very relaxed last night. That was the best sex we've ever had. What got a hold of you?"

"I don't know," Matt answered. "All I know is that I felt my knee tingle, then the next thing I know we were rocking and rolling."

"Well," she responded. "If we keep that up, we will be parents soon." "If we do, it will be all part of the plan."

"Part of God's plan," she answered and gave him a peck on his forehead. "You know our Pastor spoke yesterday about how God has a plan for all of us. In the book of Jeremiah, chapter twenty-nine, verse eleven, God says to Jeremiah,

"For I know the plans I have for you, declares the Lord, plans to prosper you and not to harm you, plans to give you home and a future."

"That means God has a plan for all of us." "Yeah, I know what he said," Matt responded.

"But you know it looks like we see more bad than good."

"Pastor also talked about how the devil has his own plans, and we must be strong and fight against those plans of the devil."

"Let me read something to you," she picked up her Bible and turned to the book of Ephesians.

"Ephesians chapter six, verse eleven says,

"Put on the full armor of God, so that you can take your stand against the devil's schemes."

"You will learn more about all the armor God equips us with to use against evil. The devil doesn't play fair, and he uses many devices."

"Verse twelve says,"

"For our struggle is not against flesh and blood, but against the rulers, against the authorities, against the powers of this dark world and against the spiritual forces of evil in the heavenly realms."

"Okay," Matt said, as he reached and closed Tangie's Bible.

"I'm trying to make sense of this good versus evil thing. Let me keep going at my speed. If your God has a plan for me, or for us, then let's see what happens."

"We also have to do our parts, with good guidance." She answered. "The devil is working twenty-four-seven to make us follow his evil schemes. But God is also working with us twenty-four-seven to help keep us on the path of righteousness."

"We pray for discernment between the two."

"And speaking of plans, you know I have a doctor's appointment today. It is long overdue. It will probably be all day because I will see more than one doctor. I have so many things to have checked out."

"What do you have planned for today?" "I plan to work on your car today."

"You take the other car. I had this strange dream last night about that strange object Flo gave us."

"I dreamt that I installed that part into the engine of your car. I'm going to mess around with your engine a bit and see if that part has any relationship with your engine. You know I think that car has some effect on that part."

"Maybe it was a leftover part from experimental electric motors," she said.

"For all we know they could have developed or engineered electric vehicles right there in our facility."

"Just don't get yourself electrocuted," she said with a wry smile. As Matt said goodbye to his wife, his phone rang.

"Hello," he answered.

"Hey Matt, this is your golfing buddy Greg. How you doing?" "Hey Greg. How are you, and to what do I owe this call?"

"Clark and I are playing golf today, and wanted to know if you can join us. We could use some tips from your newfound golfing expertise."

"Thanks for the invite, Greg, but I made other plans for today. Looks like y'all are getting in some bonus golf. Do y'all plan to play golf again this week?"

"We plan to play again Wednesday while the wives are cooking the Thanksgiving meals."

"I can play with you guys then."

"Okay, Matt. We'll see you Wednesday. By the way, did you see this morning's newspaper?"

"No. What's in it?"

"You're in it," Greg said in a happy tone.

"Me?" Matt questioned in a very surprised tone. "Yes. Your name, at least."

"I have a nephew who works at the newspaper. I told him about you recommending a diet of only milk and water drinking to control nightmares, and he wrote an article about it."

"It has a heading, 'Cure for Nightmares May Be Found In Your Kitchen.'"

"That's very interesting," Matt responded, "but there's no scientific studies to back that up."

"Doesn't matter," Greg responded back. "It works for me. Maybe it can help someone else."

"How much did you say about me?" Matt asked, as he started to wonder how much public knowledge was divulged about his life.

"I just gave him your name, and told him you are a scientist who works for Los Alamos," Greg answered.

Matt slapped his head, and silently said, *Oh no!* to himself, thinking the last thing he wanted was his name and information about him printed in the paper.

He quickly gathered himself, knowing he should not show any negative emotional reaction to Greg because he had provided Greg the information, and did not tell him not to use it.

"Okay," he said to Greg in a calm voice.

"Maybe it will help someone else. I'll see you Wednesday."

Matt stood silently for a few minutes, wondering to himself if he had inadvertently provided information that may violate his employer's policy.

He spoke out to himself.

"Man! The last thing I needed was my name in the paper. Well, Greg didn't know. And this will probably have no effect on anything."

"Let me get to my car."

He picked up the spark plug looking device and headed to the garage.

As before, the object started vibrating, and felt a little warm in Matt's hand as he approached the car.

He raised the hood of the car and started examining the engine.

He examined the power electronics controller, then the power inverter. Between the two parts was a small hole. Matt wondered if the part in his hand would fit into the hole. He believed this was the area he could insert the object, as he had seen in his dream.

He stuck the object into the hole, and the object began a dim glow. Matt's eyes lit up. He got into the car and started the engine. The engine sounded more powerful than before. He got out and looked at the car.

"Okay," he said, as he nodded his head in approval of what appeared a more powerful engine.

"At least the new part didn't hurt anything. It seems to have helped make the car better."

He turned off the engine, closed the hood, and went back into the house to get a snack.

Later that evening, Tangie returned home. She came into the living room where Matt was taking a nap.

She was crying. She ran to him on the couch and grabbed him.

"What's wrong, honey?" he asked as she wrapped her arms around him. "The doctor told me that I'm barren. I can't have children," she said

while still crying.

"You mean infertile?" he asked. "Yes!"

"She said I must have become that way because of the intense physical activity I have put on my body. That must have affected my ability to ovulate. My physical activities must have had a detrimental effect on my fallopian tubes or uterus."

"Is there anything that can be done to correct it?" he asked. "There are treatments such as medications and even surgery."

"We will discuss the remedies next visit. She wanted me to discuss with you first."

"We will do whatever we need to do." he answered, as he held her and tried to comfort her and ease her hurt.

"Even if we have to adopt, we will do whatever it takes to have a family."

CHAPTER

24

BACK TO WORK

Matt sat down in front of the cage as the doors in front of the cage opened, and Poker the goat walked out.

Matt starting deep breathing techniques, and began a self-hypnotic routine.

As he fell into his trance, a vision of him laying strapped to a table looking up flashed in his mind.

He quickly jumped back into consciousness and looked around. He looked at Poker, who just stood there chewing.

He started to return back into his hypnotic state. As he fell into a deeper state, he had another flash. He saw himself lying strapped and looking around in a dimly lit room.

This flash scared him awake again. Again, he looked around. He looked at Poker. He decided not to go back into the relaxed state again that day.

The next day, he decided to attempt to communicate with Poker without going into any trancelike state.

He looked at the goat, trying to communicate with just his conscious mind. Poker did not respond, and did not respond to his conscious communication the rest of the week.

The next week, he decided to return to his self-induced hypnosis and fight through the visions that were interrupting his communication with his goat.

As he relaxed, another vision flashed into his mind.

He was back on the table strapped down. He could see two figures in the dimly lit room looking back at him.

Again, this experience woke him from his trancelike state.

He started pondering the visions he was seeing. He sat there the remainder of the day trying to figure out what he was experiencing.

For the rest of the day and the remainder of the week, he became more interested in trying to figure out his flashbacks than advancing any interaction with his goat.

He knew he could not discuss his experience with Tangie, as he knew he was forbidden from discussing any work-related issues with anyone.

CHAPTER

25

FLASHBACKS COME HOME

At the end of the week, something happened that made Matt talk to Tangie about his visions.

On that Friday night, he dozed off in his bed at home. Tangie had already fallen asleep.

As he fell into a deeper state of sleep, a vision of him lying strapped on the table in the dimly lit room came to him.

In this vision, he looked up through the dim light and saw two figures with large heads looking at him.

He immediately woke up and sat up in bed. His action woke Tangie up. "What's wrong, baby?" she asked. "Are you having a nightmare?"

"I must be!" he answered in a cold sweat.

"You mean your milk and water diet is not preventing you from having bad dreams?"

"No. That is not a proven remedy. That's our theory."

"Milk may actually have contributed to my vision. You know milk relaxes the body, which relaxes the brain. This could lead to a greater state of dreaming. That greater state might occasionally lead to a nightmare or at least some visions."

"But it was more like a flashback than a nightmare, although both can result from a bad experience. I can't think of any bad experience that would cause me nightmares," he said, with a dumbfounded look on his face."

"Okay," she responded while she rubbed his back. "Just go back to sleep."

"Good thing the weekend is coming up. Relax and think about playing golf with your buddies."

"You're right. I just need to relax."

They both laid back down, and tried to relax.

About twenty minutes later, Matt dozed back off to sleep. In his sleep, he had another flashback.

He had a flashback of being strapped on a table and opening his eyes and seeing two alien beings looking down at him.

This time Matt let out a yell, and sat up in bed with a terrified look on his face.

Tangie popped up, awaked by his yell.

"What's going on with you!" she asked, in a very concerned tone.

"I had a flashback of two extraterrestrial humanoid beings looking down at me!" he said in an excited state. Then he looked at her.

"I believe this means that you were right about the existence of UFOs and aliens."

"Why do you think you are having nightmares about aliens? Do you think you have had an encounter with an alien?"

"I believe we were abducted," he answered.

"We must have been abducted that night were driving to Roswell from Fort Sumner."

"That would explain the lights that came up behind us. That would explain how we woke up on side of the road. That would explain the extra time it took us to get to Roswell."

"What do you think they did to us?" she asked. "I don't know."

"I don't feel any differently. Have you noticed anything different in either of us?"

"Not really. I don't feel any differently. If we were abducted, it hasn't affected me yet."

"But it makes sense that if they abduct people, they would do it on lonely, dark highways where nobody else is around."

"Many people recall their abduction experiences when they undergo hypnosis. Maybe when we go to the orphanage in a couple weeks to take kids Christmas presents, we can get Flo to put you into a deep hypnotic state."

"Maybe we can get more information from a session with her. She's a certified hypnotist, and she's very good at everything she does. I believe she can get you to recall that night in great detail."

"I guess I can give it a try."

"Maybe she can also help me turn off these UFO nightmares."

26

CONTACT FROM A STRANGER

On Friday evening, Tangie sat home at her computer going through the internet researching information on infertility when her screen went out.

On the screen appeared an unknown man. His face was covered with a mask. He had on a black hood. The background behind him was dark. "Hello, Tangie and Matt," the stranger greeted in a digitally disguised voice.

Tangie looked at her screen with a very surprised expression on her face. Matt rose up from reading a magazine on the sofa, and walked over to the computer.

"Who are you?" Tangie asked. "How do you know us?"

"I'll tell you that later," the stranger answered. "I need to meet with you two."

"Why?" Matt asked.

"I need to talk to you about your jobs."

"I know you work for G.O.D., and I know what you do."

"It's very important that I talk to you." "When and where?" Matt asked.

"I'm in Southern California. I know where you are. Let's meet about halfway in Tucson, the day after New Year's Day. I'll call you again before then about a time and place."

"You expect us to feel safe meeting you?" Tangie asked.

"We will meet in a public place in the daytime with people around," the stranger answered.

"We will meet in the daytime, because I do not travel at night out of the city."

The stranger then signed off.

"That was weird," Tangie said, with a puzzled look at Matt. "What was that all about?"

"I don't know, but it looks like our jobs are not as secret as we thought."

27

CHRISTMAS VISIT TO THE ORPHANAGE

"Wow!" Tangie said to Matt, as she watched him cram in the last of the Christmas gifts into their EV.

"We needed the SUV for all of the gifts we have for the kids." "Yeah," Matt agreed.

"And I got a map of all of the charging stations on the way."

"I don't think we will make it all the way to Albuquerque on one charge. We may have to recharge again before we arrive. With all of these gifts I figure we will need three or four recharges on this trip."

"This works out great," Tangie said, as they drove off.

"We visit the orphanage a few days before Christmas so the kids will have gifts in time for Christmas. And we get to see our families on Christmas day."

"Every Christmas is different," Matt added.

"Flo gives us a list of the kids' needs. Their needs change as they get older. And we get somebody new every year."

"Well Jamie is not new," she added. "And I got a special gift for him."

"I believe I've made progress with him since our first visit. I plan to see him today. And I anticipate he will respond to me."

"I kinda wish we could be there on Christmas Day to see the kids open their gifts and see the smiles on their faces, but then they would know where the gifts came from. Some do believe in Santa Clause, and we don't want to spoil that."

"Speaking of responses," Matt intervened, changing the subject.

"I'm wondering about the strange man who contacted us for a meeting.

I don't expect wonderful news as it pertains to our jobs." "I'm curious also," she added.

"Our jobs are full of surprises. And that's about all we can discuss about our jobs."

"Do you think we are risking our lives meeting with this man?"

"I have to be honest, I'm not sure. I just feel we have to meet him or something may happen later on that could be a big surprise."

Four and a half hours after the couple left Carlsbad, they arrived at Flo's Grace and Peace orphanage.

"We're here," Matt said as they drove through the gate. "And we didn't have to recharge the car," Tangie added.

"Maybe the extra weight from all those gifts had little effect on the battery," Matt said.

"Maybe these EV batteries are better than advertised."

Flo smiled and waved at the couple as they rode up and parked at the main building.

"Welcome! And Merry Christmas!" Flo yelled, as the couple exited the vehicle.

"Merry Christmas to you!" they both called back, as they walked up to give Flo a hug.

"It's so good to see y'all!" Flo said. "It's great to be here," Matt said. "Yes, it is!" Tangie added.

"We better get the gifts unloaded," Matt said. "Yes," Flo agreed.

"And God bless you two for being so generous. We can take them to the day room now while no one is in there. I made sure to clear it out until this evening. I know y'all don't want the kids to see Santa before Christmas."

After about twenty minutes, they put the last gifts under the huge Christmas tree in the dayroom.

"I believe we have something for everyone according to your list," Matt said to Flo.

"I know you have. Ever since y'all told me you love Christmas shopping, you have taken the baton and ran with it.

"We enjoy it," Tangie added.

"I know we don't plan to be here Christmas Eve or Christmas Day, and we didn't want the kids to see us unloading the presents today, but can I see Jamie before we leave?"

"Of course!" Flo answered.

"I also have a request of you Flo," Matt said. "What is it?"

"I have been having some strange dreams or flashbacks."

"So, you have had some type of stressful experience that you believe is triggering these flashbacks?"

"Yes."

"Can you relate the flashback?" "Yes, I can."

"We believe it relates to the evening when we visited Fort Sumner. We were driving to Roswell after our tour of the Billy the Kid Museum." "It became dark as we were driving on that straight road from Fort

Sumner. We saw a light approaching."

"Next thing we know, we're waking up on side of the road. At first, we thought we had stopped for a nap because we had spent all day in Fort Sumner and were tired."

"But now, Flo, I think we were abducted." "Really?"

"Yes," Matt answered.

"We can't account for the time it took us to drive from Fort Sumner to Roswell."

"That's about a two-hour drive at most. It took us five hours. I don't believe we slept for three hours."

"Wow!" Flo exclaimed.

"What do you want me to do?"

"I want a hypnotherapy session with you. I want to determine and confirm what we experienced that night."

"These flashbacks are disturbing my sleep. Maybe hypnosis will help stop the nightmares."

"Okay," Flo responded.

"We can go to my office. Since I use hypnosis on some residents here, I have a comfortable sofa in my office."

"I'll visit with Jamie while you two are having your session," Tangie said. "Where is he, Flo?"

"In his usual spot down the hall," Flo answered. "Okay, I'll catch up with y'all in a bit."

Tangie walked from the dayroom to the inner hallway, while Flo and Matt headed the opposite way to go to her office.

Tangie approached Jamie, who sat on the floor in the hallway leading to the dayroom. She knelt down and spoke to him.

"Hello Jamie," she called to him.

Jamie didn't say anything. He moved his head slightly but kept looking away.

"It's so good to see you again. I was looking forward to it," she paused for a reaction. Jamie didn't react. She then continued.

"I want to wish you a merry Christmas."

"I also want to say that I really want to communicate with you. And I believe you want to communicate with me. And I'm here for you."

Flo and Matt entered her office.

"Those familiar words," Flo said to him. "Why don't you lie down on my sofa?"

"Okay," Matt responded with a smile, and made himself comfortable on the sofa chair next to the office back wall.

"I'm going to record this session, so you will know what you said during the session," she said as she picked up a recorder.

"That's fine with me."

"Now," Flo said, as she pulled up a chair next to the sofa chair.

"I want you to close your eyes and first go through all of the relaxation processes you use to relax your mind if you apply any self-hypnotic techniques. If you do not have a self-hypnotic routine, then just go through your routine of relaxing and going to sleep each night."

Matt closed his eyes and relaxed into the sofa.

"You're going to be more comfortable starting with your relaxation steps," Flo said in a soothing voice. "Now we transition to you concentrating on me."

"I want you to picture in your mind how you look relaxing on this sofa. You are looking down at yourself in a very relaxed state. You are getting very comfortable on this sofa. You want to relax and fall asleep."

"You want to think about your life." "Remember your life as a child." "Picture your favorite toys."

"Now picture when you first started school." "Remember what you wore to school." Matt's eyes rolled under his eyelids.

"Now remember when your dad took you to the firing range." "Picture the gun he put in your hand."

She paused.

"Now remember when you started college." "Picture the papers you signed to get into college." "Remember your college graduation."

"Now let's go to your wedding day."

"Picture how Tangie looked walking down the aisle." "Now let's go to you and Tangie moving to New Mexico." "Picture moving into your house."

"Now picture the places you have visited in New Mexico."

"Now remember visiting Fort Sumner. Think of the things you saw at Fort Sumner."

"Now talk to me, Matt."

"Can you remember you and Tangie getting in your car and leaving Fort Sumner?"

"Yes," Matt answered.

"Do you remember when it turned dark as you were driving from Fort Sumner to Roswell?"

"Yes," he answered. "Now talk to me Matt."

Tell me about the light approaching your car as you were driving. "The light came up to the car," he started his remembrance. "The light stopped over the car."

"What happened next?" Flo asked.

"Our car is slowing down and turning onto the side of the road. I'm trying to keep driving, but the car is stopping on the side of the road."

He continued.

"The car doors open by themselves. Tangie and I are floating out of the car and up into a spacecraft hovering over the car. "We are floating into an open door at the bottom of the craft."

Matt started gasping.

"Please calm down, and continue," Flo commanded.

"Several gray alien beings with large heads and large eyes are waiting on us in the craft."

"They are grabbing us and strapping us down on tables."

"Different colored lights are pulsating from the straps. Red, green, white."

"What happened next?" Flow asked.

"Two of the aliens are looking at me," he answered. "I can't move."

"I am scared, but I am calm."

"They are looking at me as if they want to talk to me, but they don't have mouths."

"I am asking them questions in my mind about where they came from, how they traveled, and what is their purpose here. They are answering telepathically because they have no mouths."

"Next I am waking up back in our car."

"Okay, Matt you can wake up," Flo commanded in a loud tone. Matt's eyes opened, and he sat up.

"I feel exhausted," he said, as he slumped over.

"You definitely had an extraordinary experience between Fort Sumner and Roswell," Flo stated to him.

"You talked about how you and Tangie floated out of your car and into a spacecraft."

"You said gray alien beings were in the spaceship, and that you communicated with them."

"I'll play back what you said." She turned on the recorder.

"This experience has made me believe in extraterrestrial beings," he stated.

"I was not a believer before."

"And it looks like they are much more advanced than we are."

"I can see where you would have flashbacks from that experience," Flo said.

"But you should not have any more flashbacks now that the source of those flashbacks has been revealed."

"Thank you, Flo," he said in a relieved tone. "But I wonder what they wanted with us." "Makes sense to me," Flo answered.

"You and Tangie are very intelligent people. If those creatures like studying people, why not abduct and examine smart people? And why not abduct when they have an excellent opportunity on a lonely road."

"Now tell me, Matt. Other than the nightmares, have you or Tangie felt any differently physically or mentally?"

"Not that I can tell."

"The only thing I have noticed is that my knee tingles sometimes. But I think that comes from the horse-riding accident I had when I was a kid. I figured my knee might start affecting me at some point."

"It's not a debilitating effect. Just a tingle so far."

"Well," Flo responded, "you know there are stories of abductees having chips implanted into their bodies when they are abducted. You may want to have a thorough examination of your body for any foreign objects."

"I think I will," he answered.

Tangie continued her relentless attempt to communicate with Jamie. She moved closer to him and bent her head over to try to look him in his eyes. Jamie moved his head slightly and turned his eyes to meet her eyes. She starred back at him, feeling that he was finally ready to say some-

thing to her.

But instead of opening his mouth, he looked into her eyes, and she felt him communicate with her.

"They took my dad!" She felt him communicate to her telepathically. Then he turned his head away from her and looked back down again.

She absorbed his statement, rolling her eyes and blinking, wondering what he meant. She knew he was not ready to say anything else.

"Okay, Jamie," she said as she stood up.

"It's time for me to go. I'll see you again soon. Have a very merry Christmas."

"Did you two make any progress? Tangie asked as she approached Matt and Flo.

"Yes," Matt answered.

"We were definitely abducted."

"They examined us. I asked them questions about how they got here, and their purpose, and they answered my questions."

"What is their purpose?" Tangie asked.

"They said they want to help mankind build a more peaceful existence.

They said they want to help us. Flo has our session recorded."

"I'd be very suspicious of anything that looks ungodly," Flo chimed in. "If God's hand isn't in it, then it's evil."

"You know we cannot tell anyone about our experience. I say our experience because I know if Flo examines you under hypnosis, you will confirm the abduction."

"I agree," Tangie said.

"Maybe I will have a session at some point. I want to know exactly what happened to me."

"How did your meeting with Jamie go?" Flo asked Tangie. "Very well," Tangie answered.

"I believe we are beginning to connect. I really look forward to working with him."

"Great!" Flo said in a loud voice.

"You may be the answer to my prayers for him."

28

ANOTHER ABDUCTION ATTEMPT

M att, you won't believe what happened with my visit with Jamie," Tangie said, as they drove back home from the orphanage.

"What?"

"He actually communicated with me," she said. "And it was a telepathic communication." "Really?"

"Yes."

"And we can talk about it because it is not work related. But I didn't want to tell Flo everything just yet. She has her own way of working with him. I didn't want to make it look like I'm taking her place."

"I wouldn't be too concerned about that," Matt said.

"I actually believe Flo wants you and me to take some of the work with him off her. I think she wants him to be our project."

"Maybe so," Tangie agreed.

"But I want to be very thoughtful of her."

"I finally got him to turn and look into my eyes."

"And he said without opening his mouth 'They took my dad.' Then he turned away, not wanting to communicate anymore."

"That could mean," Matt analyzed, "that he was separated from his dad, probably by force."

"Then his father could be out there somewhere." She said.

"I believe he will eventually provide more information. Maybe Flo can hypnotize him and get his story, although he would need to be a willing subject for a successful hypnotherapy session."

"Yeah," Matt responded.

"You would probably need to make more progress with him, and gain more of his trust."

"I think I can also say, without specifically talking about our jobs, that you seem to be progressing just fine to be able to communicate with Jamie like that."

"I don't know."

"To be honest, I didn't think I was progressing that much. And I guess that's about all we can say about our jobs right now."

"But we can talk about Jamie, as he becomes more prominent in our lives."

They drove on toward home. Day had turned to night, since the couple spent most of the day at the orphanage.

"We're only about fifty miles from home, and the indicator light says the battery on this EV is still fully charged." Matt said, as he looked at the instrument panel on the dashboard.

"Matt," she responded, "there's no other way to explain that except the metallic spark plug you installed into this car is giving it the extra battery life."

"I believe so."

"We've driven over a thousand miles without a recharge. There's no EV that can go that far without recharging. I'm not even counting the miles we put on the car before this trip."

"In fact, we haven't recharged the battery since I installed that plug." "If that is the reason," Tangie added, "there's no telling what technology that is going on in the higher levels of our facility."

"It's probably like they do a lot of products. They already have the next phone, computer, or whatever, when they are trying to get sufficient sales from the one they are currently advertising."

"It makes me even more anxious to see what else is on the upper levels."

"What are we going to do about letting people know about this new device?" She asked.

"We take it one step at a time."

"First, we need to confirm that the device is actually the cause of the additional power. I will take it out and see how far the car goes without it." "Then we still have to keep it a secret for a while. We are technically not supposed to have that device. We need to actually have fourth level access even before we can begin a process of using the right procedures to manufacture this device and get it into every EV."

"I feel my knee tingling. I call it tingling because it doesn't hurt. It just feels like a nerve there is receiving additional stimulation."

"Maybe it's a sign of something," Tangie commented. "God is always trying to get our attention in some way."

"So, you think my knee feelings are God trying to tell me something?" he asked in a skeptical tone.

"Could be."

"The Bible says God moves in mysterious ways. Those can be ways we don't understand at the time. But God understands."

Tangie looked back out of the passenger side window. She saw lights moving in the sky.

"Matt, I see lights in the sky again!" she said as she sat up.

"Looks like they are moving. Looks like some kind of moving objects." "Are the lights coming toward us?" he asked.

She looked intently at the lights.

"I think they are moving our way," she continued starring at the lights. Matt glanced out her window.

"Yes, they are definitely coming toward us!" she said in a frightened voice.

"They might be UFOs! They could be coming for us again!" "Artesia is a few miles ahead," Matt responded.

"Maybe if we get into town they will go away." "Speed up," she yelled.

Matt pushed the pedal down on the vehicle. They passed a sign that read "Artesia 5 Miles." "Speed up!" Tangie yelled again.

"They are getting closer!"

"I'm flooring it!" Matt yelled back, as the speedometer went up to the limit.

"I just hope they don't shut down the engine!" "Faster!" She yelled.

"They're coming up fast!

"Faster! Faster!" she commanded.

"I'm going as fast as I can!" he yelled back as he looked at the sign that read "Artesia City Limits."

"They're almost here!" she cried out in panic.

She saw a beam of light come from one of the spaceships toward them. "God help us!" she screamed.

Just as the beam of light was almost at the car, they drove into the city lights and the town of Artesia. They could see people walking on the street sidewalks. The spacecrafts turned away and disappeared into the sky.

Some people turned and looked at the speeding car. Matt slowed down as he passed a sign that read, "Speed Limit 35."

He pulled the car over to the curb and put the car in Park. They both let out deep breaths.

"That was close." Tangie said, in a relieved tone. "They almost had us again."

"Yeah," Matt agreed, as he breathed heavily. "I'm exhausted."

"Look, there's a saloon," he pointed to the establishment a half block ahead of where they had parked.

"Let's go get something to drink and calm down. Right now, I feel like I could drink anything."

"And then we need to get a place to stay here tonight," she added.

"I don't think we should be driving at night on those lonely dark roads." "Yes," Matt agreed.

The couple walked into the saloon, and up to the bar. Three Caucasian men with scraggly beards men sitting at a table with their drinks stopped drinking and looked at the strangers entering their hangout.

"I'll have a bottled water," Tangie called to the bartender. "Same for me," Matt followed.

One of the men at the table stood up and walked to the couple. The other two men stood up at their table.

He walked up beside Tangie.

"You mean a pretty little thang like you is only drinking water?" he said to her, in a country twang.

Matt stood up off his stool.

"Easy, cowboy!" the man said to Matt.

"I'm just trying to be hospitable and offer your gal something nice and tasty."

"She knows what she wants," Matt answered.

"Wait Matt," she said to Matt, as she turned around to face the man. "Let me answer the gentleman."

"Thanks for your offering, sir, but it's been a long day, and we just need some nice cold water. Thanks for your offering," she turned back around and faced the bartender.

"I'm trying to be nice, bitch!" he said. He reached to grab her arm.

Before he could touch her, she blocked his arm. Then she kicked him back. The bartender stood frozen by what he was watching.

The man looked a little surprised. Then he gathered himself and prepared to retaliate.

One of his buddies at the table ran over and grabbed Matt from be- hind, and wrapped his arms around Matt, as he and his other buddy at the table anticipated his friend would strike back at Tangie.

The first man ran back to Tangie, preparing to strike her. She sidestepped him, elbowed him in his ribs, and karate chopped him at the back base of his neck. He fell flat on the floor.

Matt back-kicked the man that held him between the man's legs in his groin. The man let Matt go and grabbed his groin, moaning in pain. Matt then gave him a strong uppercut in the face. The man fell backward and flattened a table to the floor. He was out cold.

The third man at the table just looked in shock.

Tangie leaned over to the man she had knocked on the floor. He was in pain. He raised his head up.

She bent over him.

"The trouble with you good old boys," Tangie said to him, "is that you are good at drinking and good at disrespecting women. But you are usually not very good at fighting."

She punched him in the face and knocked him out cold.

Matt threw a twenty-dollar bill at the bartender.

"Keep the change," Matt said, as he grabbed the bottled waters, and he and Tangie walked out of the bar.

About twenty minutes later, they checked into a local motel.

"I can't believe what just happened," Tangie said, as she walked into the room and fell backwards onto the bed.

"What?" Matt asked, as he closed the motel door. "That aliens tried to abduct us again, or the bar fight?" "Both!" she answered.

"I mean, this is the first time I've ever had to use my martial arts training in actual self-defense. It's like I've been training my whole life for this moment. It felt unreal but so natural. I was scared, but I was prepared."

"I'm proud of you," he said.

"And I wasn't bad, thanks to the training I got from you."

"You were excellent," she said to him, as she raised up and kissed him. "It actually felt good, like an adrenaline rush. Think of what brain

process our minds went through over the past hour or so." "Yeah," Matt answered.

"Chemical, electrical, and physical actions and reactions. Neurons firing all over. Fight or flight processes going on."

"Aliens and rednecks. What an experience."

"And I think that spark plug in the engine may have kept the aliens from shutting down the power in the car, and allowed us to make it."

"I give God the credit," she said. "God and the spark plug," he added.

"And what about getting into trouble in the first place? Nothing like this has ever happened to us."

"Jesus said we would have trials and tribulations in this evil world." she answered.

"But He also equips us with what we need to overcome problems. He does not allow more than we can handle. And I believe he is equipping you. Just like He did for Saul, who became the great Saint Paul."

"I believe there's something to that tingle in your knee. Something is happening. It seems to happen just before something else happens."

"You know we were abducted. No telling what the aliens did to us. And it looks like they want us again."

"Let's get your knee examined when we get back home. It is reported that the aliens insert chips in people. These chips probably are used to monitor people. They probably are even used to control people. Maybe even control their offspring."

"I can see where those aliens would be very interested in us and our facility. It's a secret facility. Many UFO sightings have been around military installations. I can see where they would be very interested in a quasi-military secret facility."

"We've probably been targets from the beginning," he responded. "They have been looking for the right opportunities to abduct us.

That's when we're not around other people, and at night." "I'll get an examination when we get back home." "We'll leave when the sun comes up."

CHAPTER

29

KNEE EXAMINATION

"The X-ray scan definitely shows a small clump just in front of your articular cartilage, and above the meniscus," Matt's doctor said to him in the hospital examination room. Matt sat on the examination

bed. Tangie stood in the room. "I thought so," Tangie said.

"It's right behind your patellar tendon," the doctor continued, as he held up the pictures of the scan sheets to the light board.

"It's a foreign object. Isn't it?" Matt asked the doctor. "Yes, I believe so."

"Looks like you've had some type of surgery here before?" "It was more a stitching procedure," Matt answered.

"When I fell off a horse as a kid, I landed mainly on this knee. I just stretched the tendon. It was not torn. But the fall busted open the skin, and it was stitched back. The stitches make it look like I had a serious knee operation."

"We told you why we wanted the knee scanned. Now I want to get that object out and see what it looks like. And I want it examined."

"I can schedule the surgery tomorrow," the doctor answered.

"You'll use crutches for traveling home after the surgery. Stay off the leg for a week. Then we will see if you need any physical therapy."

"Doctor Schinn, have you ever seen anything like this before?" Tangie asked.

"Not really. And I know where you are coming from with that question."

"I've heard about chips being extracted from people who claim to have been abducted by aliens. I've heard some of those chips are nonmetallic, and are hard to explain."

"I'm just as interested in examining and finding out more about that chip as you all are."

"Looks like whoever inserted the chip knew exactly how to hide their evidence. They made the incision right where your scar was so it would be harder to notice that you had another surgical procedure."

"After the procedure, I'll send the chip off to Los Alamos for further examination."

"The surgery should take about two hours, maybe a little less. It depends on how well attached that thing is to you. It could be well attached to your tendons or cartilage. I just won't know how strongly attached the chip is to your body parts until we get in there."

"Rehab actually happens relatively quickly after surgery, usually within thirty-six hours."

"Do you plan to go public with your findings?" Matt asked.

"That depends on you, and depends on what the examinations and tests reveal," the doctor answered. "If the findings are inconclusive, or the chip is made of some strange but identifiable foreign material, we may want to make the international medical community aware."

"But you also risk getting the media into the circle. Network communications may give you the exposure you are not ready for. How do you feel about that?"

"I think we will take it one step at a time," Matt answered. "One simple, or I hope simple, knee surgery can turn into a complicated conundrum."

CHAPTER

30

TRIP TO MEET THE STRANGER

" "This trip to meet with this stranger in Tucson is just as intriguing and mystifying as our first day on our job," Tangie said, as they drove west from New Mexico to Arizona.

"Yeah," Matt responded. "But I don't think he is bringing us good news. My knee isn't tingling about this encounter."

"Your knee hasn't tingled since the surgery, has it?" "No."

"I agree with you that it must have been some sort of communication device implanted by the aliens. And it was helping them to keep track of us. But what about your theory that God was trying to get my attention through that device, especially if the aliens implanted it?"

"God has many ways to communicate with us." she answered.

"And I believe God was protecting you. I believe He prevented the aliens from fulfilling their mission through that chip by blocking their transmission and sending His own."

"The Bible tells us that God can take what is meant for evil and turn it into something good."

"Well, I'm proud of you."

"What are you proud of?" she asked. "Of how I handled myself in that bar fight in Artesia?"

"No. Well, yeah, I am proud of how you handled the bar fight. You were so confident of yourself in that environment. But I was talking about how you are keeping your faith through all we've gone through."

"We don't have your everyday run of the mill jobs, and you seem to be keeping everything in a good perspective."

"That's what faith does," she responded.

"Look at Flo. She worked twenty-five years underground. Seeing very few people. Faith always gives us something to hold on to."

"Well," he said. "I think you're doing a better job of that than I am." "I may be keeping the faith, but I do have questions. And I want to

ask you two of my questions, without breaking our code of silence to each other about our jobs."

"What are the questions?" he asked. "Why are we there?"

"Where?"

"There. There physically in that secret facility in a cave near Carlsbad Caverns."

"Seems like everything we've done so far could easily be carried out in any college or university anywhere in the world. I don't view anything we've done so far as that secret."

"I think mind control is very clandestine," he responded. I think the United States wants to unlock the formula first. I know it will get out eventually if we have the key to helping people help themselves."

"Maybe," she responded.

"But it makes me even more curious about the other levels in the facility, and what the end game is in this project."

"I still have questions myself," he added.

"You know I can come up with questions. But I think if we come up with a breakthrough way to help people it could be worth all of our waiting."

"Maybe so," she said.

"My second question is the same as the first. Why are we there?"

"I know God has a plan for me, and for us. But right now, I am still praying that we are doing, or going to do, something for the benefit of mankind."

"The thing about us," he commented, "is that we are not afraid to take chances. I know the money was irresistible and the chance to relocate was a dream come true, but I'd like to think we accepted the challenge of the unknown. I want to believe we not only operated on your Godly faith, but a blind faith that we can make a positive difference in this world."

"I have a feeling that this meeting today will answer many of our questions."

"And I'm anxious to know more about that chip they took from my knee. Their conclusion is inconclusive so far."

"Since it's alien technology," Tangie responded, "we may never know. If alien technology is thousands of years ahead of us, much of what they do will remain a puzzle to us."

CHAPTER

31

MEETING WITH THE STRANGER

"Here it is," Matt said as they rode into the parking lot.

"Case Natural Resource Park. I don't think we have to worry about where to find our stranger. Let's just get out and walk. He will find us."

They got out, and walked down a park walkway. A man approached them from behind.

"Mr. and Mrs. Riley," the man called, and he approached the couple and shook their hands. He had a large watch on his left arm.

"My name is Alex Six, just like the number six."

"Good to finally meet you, Mister Six," Matt said, as the couple returned his handshake.

"I work for Project Safeguard America," he informed them.

"It is a government black box project that reports directly to the NSA. Here are my credentials."

He pulled out a badge and official card of his agency. He then pushed a button on his watch and held the watch up for the couple to see the face of the watch.

A man's face appeared on the watch face.

"Hello Mr. and Mrs. Riley," the man on the watch called.

"I'm Simon Dial, Associate Director of US Affairs with the NSA. You can take my name and title and call the President of the United States if you want further verification. The president knows me."

"I want to thank you two for coming. I want you to work cooperatively with Mr. Six. I have worked with him for five years. He's a valuable asset to the NSA. And I know whatever we accomplish together will be for the benefit of America."

The watch signed off.

"Let's have a seat," Mr. Six said, as he pointed to a nearby park table and benches.

"Why did you come on our computer in a mask?" Matt asked.

"Our organization is very secretive. We don't reveal our faces until we have to meet with people. I certainly needed to meet with you two."

"We use the dark web to monitor much undercover activities. My specialty is computer hacking."

"I actually used to do what you do. I used to work for G.O.D. So, I know about your project."

"Why did you leave?" Tangie asked.

"I found out on the web and through NSA that the GOD people would eliminate me if I successfully completed Level One and Two training. I contacted the NSA because I knew through coded messages that the NSA was not being informed about operations at the facility. So, I contacted the NSA and started working with them to help them uncover the contents and intent of Level Four."

"I had to change my name and get another identity."

"I was more interested and suited for information systems and computer systems than the mind control activities of the facility. Computer hacking and spying and stealing was much more my cup of tea."

"We believe the CIA is working with top military and Space Force officials on the secret projects of Level Four. We also believe the CIA has one person supervising the Level One and Two programs, while they have another person supervise Level Four."

"They won't share information with the NSA or the president. Nor did they share information with any of the previous presidents. The NSA believes the reason is because they are planning things with their projects that neither the NSA or the president will agree with. And those plans may not be in the best interest of the national security of the United States."

"So, the NSA is going about its own way of finding out what is going on in that facility."

"The mind control is the secret project that the NSA and president does know about. It's the cover that keeps the facility open and funded as a black box project."

"But the black box segment devoted to operations like this are being funded by drug money." With the God facility, it is Columbian drug money. That is why we believe Columbians are involved with Level Five, for their own self-interest."

"So, you've been lied to about the source of your paychecks. You are being paid from drug money. But the way the facility operators look at it, they are being technically funded by the American people, since more Americans use drugs than any other country."

"Specifically, how did you find out about us?" Matt asked.

"Like I said, we have been monitoring your facility for a while. I am a computer expert, but I also keep up with news that is available to the public. When I saw the article in the local paper about how you recommended milk and water for nightmares to a local teacher, and he tied you to Los Alamos, that was the final piece of information I needed to look you up. I used that same Los Alamos cover."

"They call you the milkman at the NSA." Matt gave an incredulous look.

"What do you need with us?" Tangie asked.

"The powers that be with the NSA and other top levels of government have decided that the God facility has to go away."

"What do you mean go away?" Tangie asked.

"The facility has operated like a private corporation because they are not funded by the government, and they own the property and facility."

"The NSA and others believe there are things they have or are working on in that Fourth Level chamber that are not in the best interest of the American government or the American people."

"We abducted Mister William Moyer, the man the CIA chose to run operations on Level Four. We interrogated him and got a lot of information about Level Four, but we need more proof in order to take action."

"What happened to Mister Moyer?" Tangie asked. "That's classified information," Mr. Six answered.

"Further, we have been monitoring and trying to intercept information coming and going about Level Five. Their communication system in there is very hard to intercept and unscramble. But we do believe the people who run the facility are communicating with the Russian KGB and the Columbian government."

"We have information through wiretaps and codebreaking that the facility may be preparing to sell your information to those governments, or to operatives working for those countries. We believe there's a plan for an American abduction from one or more countries."

"If that's true," Matt interrupted, "that means they are working with foreign countries against the United States."

"We don't have one hundred percent proof of that yet. One reason is because we don't think even the CIA officials know about the Russian connection."

"It seems you want our help," Tangie surmised. "But what do you know, and what can we do?"

"I do know powerful people want the facility destroyed. But the best way for any clandestine operation will be authorized to do that is to have more concrete evidence of what is going on there, and what the facility is holding."

"I know you are working on mind control. And I know you have made a breakthrough in cracking the code to mind control."

Tangie shifted her eyes to Matt with a bit of a surprised look. He did the same to her.

"Mind control is such an unknown anomaly. We have to be sure how it is learned and used. There can be no doubt about what the situation is when people are developing or using this kind of technology."

"We need to know what you know. We need you to backup all of your work and bring it to us. You can use these electrode chip drives to record all of your work."

He handed Matt a small opaque and semi-round object with a flat side."

"Just attach this receiver key to your computer in the facility, and it will record and backup all of the work you two are doing. When you attach it, it will record all of the work you have already done."

"We also need you to go into Level Four and record what you find. When we can tie the facility's contents to their illegal plots, that will be the evidence our officials will use to destroy the facility in a covert operation." "You have to understand, there may be things in that Level Four lab that our government may believe the American people are not ready for." "There may be technological advances that many do not want out

in the market yet. The officials in government and industry who are the real power brokers do not like this much uncertainty out there that could undermine their own interests and plans."

"This is much bigger than you and me. Just trust me. You are doing the right thing."

"Talk about government and industry conspiracies," Tangie commented. "And a pissing contest between government agencies."

"We do not have clearance for Level Four," Matt stated. "How do we get in there?"

"You can get Flo to help you get in there," he answered.

"I know she is retired, but she is super intelligent. I know she went up there once when I was working with her.

"Take this translucent camera pen." He handed an object that looked like an electronic ink pen.

"Just click it and it takes 8D pictures. Hold down the clicker, and it records with sound." He handed the pen camera to Matt.

"Twist the front point of this pen, and it will freeze the security cameras for five minutes."

"It scans through doors if you cannot open the doors in that chamber." "When the objects I just gave you have the information we need, then

we can do what we need to do."

"This is a lot," Matt said. "Letting us know we have to help you help us lose our jobs."

"The NSA will offer you great jobs when this is over. The pay may not be quite as well, but you will then be able to apply more of your intelligence to doing things in a transparent manner, and in a way that will really benefit America."

"Just go to your computer and type in my last name and add three sixes when you want to communicate with me."

"What do we do first?" Tangie asked.

"Just go back to work like you normally do. And complete your mind control manual," he answered.

"Find a way to Level Four. You want to go in after hours, when you can be sure there is nobody there."

"When you get the information we need, bring it to us, and we go from there."

"We don't believe anyone has ever made it to Level Four directly from Level Two. Whoever conducts experiments and research in there does not go through Level One and Two training. And they enter the facility another way, probably through an off-limits part of the cavern."

"That's probably what that Level Three door is for," Matt surmised. "We believe they use the level training to justify what they are doing

in Level Four," Mr. Six continued.

"If they have a cover program, they can keep the funding going for the other operations going on in that complex. What better way to keep things going than to have a program they would want, but couldn't obtain?"

"There have been many mind control programs without any success. But they keep bringing in people who can make it look like the program can be successful, but it is a cover operation. The CIA and military officials probably thought mind control could not be obtained."

"Now that you have cracked the mind control code, you are in even more danger. You weren't going to make it out alive whether or not you were successful. If you had failed, they were just going to eliminate you and find someone else to keep the cover going. Now that you're successful, you are even more of a threat to them."

"One other question, Mr. Six?" Matt asked. "Yes?"

"According to Flo, you worked with another man at the facility?" Matt asked.

"Yes."

"A man named Will Knott. He left shortly after we started Level Two. He said it wasn't for him. He had a son he wanted to spend more time with after he lost his wife to a car accident. I believe he was supposed to be killed in that accident."

"I don't know what happened to him. It's like he vanished from the face of the earth. And I don't know what happened to his son either. He most likely got a new identity in order to continue living safely. The NSA helped me change my identity after I agreed to help them uncover the secrets of this facility."

"Look, no matter how things go, if you two stay there, there's a great chance you will be kidnapped or killed, or both."

"I think we got more information than we expected," Matt said to Tangie, as they rode back home.

"I'm actually not that surprised. I've learned to expect anything on this job. Now we're part of ending this facility and our jobs."

"I think it's part of a greater plan for us," Tangie stated.

"But I had a strange feeling as we met with Mr. Six. I couldn't shake that feeling."

"What did you feel like?"

"It was actually like a tingle in my body. Like the tingle in your knee before the chip was removed."

"It kind of made me feel God was trying to tell me something." "Maybe," said Matt.

"Maybe He was telling you that it was time for us to move on to a new chapter in our lives."

"Maybe. But it felt more like the serpent in the Garden of Eden tempting Adam and Eve."

"We'll see how things go," Matt concluded.

"You have such faith that your God will lead you, so what have we to fear?"

"Our God. And I am not afraid. I don't have a spirit of fear. Just common curiosity that I have faith will be answered."

32

A VISIT BACK WITH FLO

"So," Flo asked, "there's stuff and activity in that Level Four chamber that the NSA want to know about and possibly destroy because it may be used against America, or it is dangerous, or they just want

to know what's going on in there, or could be technologies that the world is not ready for?"

"That's about it," Matt answered.

"I guess that's why I felt the need to go in there," Flo responded. "But I didn't see enough to believe the thing needed shutting down." "Looks like one side of government and industry wants the research

and technology to go on and remain secret," Matt added.

"And the other side wants it exposed or terminated," Flo responded. "And they want us to find out what's in there," Tangie said.

"That's where you come in, Flo," Matt said. "Me?" Flo asked.

"Yes, you," Matt answered.

"Mr. Six believes you can get back in there. So, we need to get you back in the facility, and you need to get us in Level Four."

"We can try it," Flo responded.

"If it helps remove evil doing, then I'll do my part."

"And we found out the aliens implanted a chip in my knee," Matt added. "My doctor removed it and had it examined."

"What did your doctor find?" Flo asked.

"He said it is a type of neuromuscular substance. He sent it to Los Alamos for further study."

"We may never know the chemical or biopic makeup of the object, since the extraterrestrials are so much further advanced than we are."

33

FINAL LEVEL TWO TASK

Matt and Tangie walked through the door of Level Two, and were greeted by their voice instructor.

"Good morning, Matt and Tangie," the voice called out.

"We are starting a new phase today. We are done with the animal experiments. Your chimpanzee and goat have been anonymously donated to the Bernalillo County Petting Zoo. You can visit them any time."

"This week we start new tasks. And you will work on these programs together. No more separate work. Our spiroview brain reader that sends brain scanning waves through the room shows that both of your brains have progressed at just about the same level thus far. There is a less than a tenth of a percent difference. So, your work from here on out will be together."

"We are in the last phase of Level Two work before we schedule some volunteer human trials."

"Together you two will put together a comprehensive telepathic and mind control document. It will be a classified document that will be provided to the appropriate government officials."

"It's good to be able to talk and work together again," Tangie said to Matt as they drove home from work that afternoon.

"Yeah. I believe when we put our knowledge and experiences together, we will put together a really nice program."

"The question is who will get this paper we will write, and what are they going to do with it," Tangie retorted.

"It's just like a lot of government work," Matt answered. "You have to be on certain levels to get access or use the work. We have to chalk it up to a lot of government programs like the UFO programs. Historically in this country, top military officers, and even the President of the United States are kept out of the loop of many government programs."

"The problem I have is that I may not know if our work is for good or bad," she returned. "And I'd like to know who is benefitting from it."

"Don't know if we will ever know those things," Matt answered. "Let's just look at it as good experience as we move on and build our resumes for our careers. That's the way we have to look at it."

"Yeah, God has other plans for us, and I pray whatever we contribute will benefit mankind."

"I hope so. I just believe whatever we do and whoever we work with or work for will be more transparent than our current employer."

CHAPTER

34

LEVEL 4 VISIT

At 8 pm on Friday night, Flo entered the secret facility's atrium with Matt and Tangie. They walked to the Level 4 door. A keypad and a finger touchpad were on the wall next to the door.

"Can you get us in there?" Matt asked Flo when they reached and examined the door.

"I'm not sure," Flo answered.

"Looks like they have added a numeric keypad to the finger ID entry requirement."

Flo examined the keypad.

"I have no earthly idea what numbers and sequence of numbers will open this door," she surmised.

She held her pinky finger against the screen of the fingerprint scanner.

The scanner read, "Access Denied."

She then punched in some numbers on the keypad. The scanner again read, "Access Denied."

"This is the needle in the haystack scenario." Tangie surmised. "We may not figure this out before people return to this facility."

Flo tried several more numerical attempts without any success.

"We had to try," Matt said. "We have no choice but to keep trying. That's why we're here, to finally get to the bottom of what's going on here."

"Let's think."

"There's one other thing I can try," Flo said.

"When my coworker came down to visit me in Level One, his brain was read, just like everyone who enters that room. After he left, I read his brain components, including the physical makeup of his brain and his memory features."

"So, you are saying you studied his brain, and you know what he knows?" Tangie asked.

"I'm saying that when I studied his brain, that knowledge became part of my memory."

"Does that mean you can retrieve things from your memory that was part of his memory?" Matt asked.

"It means I can try to go back in my memory and try to retrieve what I know of his brain, and from that I may be able to get his entry code for this level."

"I firmly believe that when you access someone's brain you can then access all of their knowledge and memory."

"It's worth a try," Matt added.

Flo stepped back and shook her body, trying to relax. She stood limp. Her eyes rolled back, and she fell into a trancelike state. She stood quietly while her eyes rolled around as if she was trying to think and recall. She then closed her eyes for several minutes to increase her concentration.

She then opened her eyes, and walked to the door.

She reached up to the keypad and typed in several numbers. The pad beeped when she typed in each number. When she stopped typing in the numbers, the scanner read, "Access Granted," and the door opened.

"Wow!" Tangie reacted. "The human brain is truly remarkable." "Why did you not also need to use the touchpad?" Matt asked.

"It was just a decoy to make it look like you needed two entry processes to enter," Flo answered. "More than one entry process to any facility deters fifty percent more people from trying to break in. It doesn't have to be a real second level entry system."

They looked in and saw a long dark hallway. Matt twisted the tip of the pen, and the security cameras went blank.

They walked for about twenty-five yards down the hallway. Then they saw three closed metal doors. One door on their right, and one was on the left hallway. At the end of the hallway was a large metal door. It was much larger than the two other doors.

"We can't see what's in those rooms," Matt said. They have no windows, and are locked, with no keypad or finger scanner for opening."

"I'll hold this pen up to each door and scan them. Then let's get the heck out of here."

They walked to the first door on the left. Matt held the pen up to the door and clicked it twice. He then did the same for the door on the right. They then walked to the large door at the end of the hallway.

"This door is huge," Flo observed.

"And probably much thicker than the other two," Matt added. "I'll take a couple more clicks of it. Then let's get out of here."

35

ABDUCTION KIDNAPPERS COME CALLING

The following Monday evening, the couple returned home from work. "We're almost home," said Matt. "But why don't we go get something to eat?"

"Okay," Tangie answered. "But since we're so close to home, why don't I run in and get us something to drink? I'm thirsty, and we're so close to home I need to drink something before we get to a restaurant."

"Okay," Matt answered. "I'll run in and get us a couple of waters."

Matt parked the car outside the garage in front of the house, and ran up to the front door.

Three men with guns waited in the living room.

"Welcome, Mr. Riley," one of the men said as he pointed a gun at Matt, who froze in place.

"Where is your lovely wife?"

Matt quickly turned around and slammed the front door. He ran to the car and jumped in and sped off.

"There were men in the house waiting for us!" he said excitedly.

The three men ran to the door as Matt sped off. They ran to their car parked two houses down and sped off to follow the couple.

Matt drove fast out of town, and the men followed in their car "What do they want?" Tangie yelled.

"I just know they want us!" Matt responded.

"They are on our tail," Tangie said as she looked back.

"I'll go down Canyon Road," Matt said, and turned at a crossroad. "It's a good test of driving skills, especially at a high speed."

The men followed.

The cars screeched through winding curves.

"I don't think they intend to kill us," Matt said, as he looked back at the car approaching.

"I believe they want to kidnap us."

"I'm gonna slow down some and see if they try the PIT maneuver like when police come up and bump the backside to get a car to spin around." "That's dangerous!" Tangie yelled. "We may crash or they might

kill us."

"I think it's worth a try," Matt responded.

He reduced his speed. The chasing car came closer as they approached a curve. The car came up to the rear side of Matt's car. It started to move over to bump Matt's car.

Matt stepped on the accelerator. The chasing car missed Matt's car. It swerved off the road, busted through the guardrail, and rolled over several times. It landed at the bottom of a ravine and exploded.

Matt slowed down.

"That was close!" Tangie said, as she let out a deep breath.

"They came from somewhere and found our house and found a way to get in."

"They probably came from Columbia to smuggle us back," Matt said. "Do you think we should go back to our house?"

"Not to stay. We may have a couple days before they discover their loss and send someone else."

"That will give us some time to get some things from the house we may need."

"Those men are dead," Tangie said. "I hope they were saved."

"All I know is that we saved ourselves," Matt retorted.

"Things have changed for us. We're gonna need to hide out in different places while we figure out what's going on and who we can trust. We need to get a safety deposit box for some things. We need to store our other car. And I'm calling my dad and tell him we're gonna need some guns. I don't know how this relates to your faith, but it's what we are dealing with right now."

"Ever since that incident in the bar with those rednecks, I've been thinking," Tangie answered.

"In the Bible in the Book of Nehemiah, the Israelites were captive in Babylon. Nehemiah was a Hebrew in Persia when the word reached him that the Temple in Jerusalem was being reconstructed. He prayed to God to use him to save the city. God answered his prayer. The Persian king, Artaxerxes, then gave Nehemiah his blessing and also supplies to be used to rebuild the walls of Jerusalem. Nehemiah was made governor of the project when he returned."

"But there were enemies of Jerusalem who did not want the city rebuilt. They were the Arabs, the Ammonites, and the Ashdodites. They conspired to destroy Jerusalem. So, Nehemiah had half his workers constructing the city, while the other half held shields, spears, bows, and wore armor for protection. The Bible said every builder had his sword girded to his side as he built."

"I don't have a problem fighting for protection."

36

INFORMATION TO MR. SIX AND MR. DIAL

The couple met again with Mr. Six at a hotel in Tucson. Mr. Dial was on a screen monitor communicating from his office in Washington DC. "You were right about someone wanting us," Matt said to the men when they entered the hotel room.

"Three men were at our house when we came home. We managed to get away in our car. They crashed and were killed chasing us."

"I expected someone to come after you," Mr. Six responded.

"They will try again until you are captured or killed," Mr. Dial added. "And most likely they want you alive until they get what they want."

"We're on the run now," Tangie added.

"We're staying in different places until we get things sorted out."

Don't worry," Mr. Dial responded. "We're going to provide you a safe house, and you can stay there while you're transitioning to go to work for the

NSA. The house is fairly remote, with all kinds of sensors and cameras around it."

"Even if you go to work somewhere else you can still stay in the safe house long as you want to."

"Since you have learned mind control, the CIA cannot maintain their cover of Level Four. This may now trigger their plans for what they plan to do with the contents of that chamber."

"Now, do you have the information we need?" Mr. Six asked. "Yes," Matt answered, as he handed the pen to him.

Mr. Six took the pen and walked over to a monitor.

They all sat down facing the screen. He plugged the pen into the machine. The screen came on. He brought the screen monitor Mr. Dial was on over so he could see the screen. He tapped the pad.

"Let's see what's behind door number one," Mr. Six said.

He touched a few keys. An image of what appeared to be a small air conditioner unit appeared on the screen. It was about two feet high. It had what looked like a solar panel on top of the unit.

"Just what I thought," Mr. Six declared. "This is a solar blast sygnonometer, designed from alien technology. It can generate electricity from sunlight instantly, and send out electric waves up to five thousand miles. It makes the use hydroelectric plants obsolete. It can send power to any electrical device, thus eliminating the need for power lines, power cords, and electric outlets. This would put millions of people and lots of businesses and utility companies out of work."

"This confirms the existence of the device," Mr. Dial added. "We knew there was a secret company called America First, a secret private utility company, looking to patent this technology. Mr. Moyer was president of this company."

"But there are several companies and CIA and military officials who want to use this device for their own purposes. And there are others who don't want that device to see the light of day."

"I gather the abduction of Mr. Moyer has slowed down operations on Level Four?" Matt asked.

"Probably," Mr. Six answered. "Operations may have even stopped for now. Moyer's absence has set the company back from pursuing its patent and getting this device pushed any farther."

"Why would anybody want to keep this device secret?" Tangie asked. "This is the kind of technology that would benefit mankind."

"The problem is that the waves generated from this machine can also kill everyone within a five-thousand-mile radius," Mr. Six answered.

"Many powerful people are not ready to make this technology known. They want their companies to keep on making money as long as they can, while they figure out how to make money themselves from this technology."

"It's just like many companies who sit on the newest phone or television while they sell the older ones. The only caveat is that this technology has a deadly side effect."

"Let's go to door number two," Mr. Six said, as he tapped the keypad on his device.

The screen showed an image of a large gun that looked like a cross between a bazooka and a water gun.

"That's the death wave cadmium gun prototype," Mr. Dial said.

"That thing is designed to shoot an invisible heat wave through walls without damaging the walls, and destroy its target by setting it on fire from the insides and making the target spontaneously combust. It can shoot its wave around, over, or under obstacles like mountains and bodies of water if necessary to get to its target."

"It's a weapon mankind is not ready for."

The screen also showed images of various small metal looking objects scattered all about the room.

"Looks like they could be pieces of alien spacecrafts," Matt stated. "Yes," Mr. Six responded. "But also, useable parts, like the part that

powers your car."

"This must be where the man worked that visited Flo," Tangie stated. "He brought her that spark plug looking piece and asked her to analyze it. She gave it to us. On a strong hunch Matt installed it into our electric car engine. And since he did that, we haven't had to charge the car battery."

"That's just a sample of the kind of technology in that facility," Mr. Six replied. "Now, let's go to the big door." He clicked the keyboard. "The images will be fuzzy because the door is so thick."

The three of them moved their heads closer to the monitor trying to make out what they were looking at.

"It's a huge room," Tangie declared. "Looks like an airplane hangar."

"Yes," Mr. Six agreed. "And those five fuzzy objects look like alien aircraft pieces."

"One of the objects looks like a big piece of the alien spacecraft that crashed near Roswell, New Mexico in nineteen forty seven."

"That bell shaped, acorn looking image might be the UFO that crashed near Kecksburg, Pennsylvania in nineteen sixty five. We believe it is a time machine capable of transporting anyone to any time in history. Very intriguing."

"We have all the information we need," Mr. Dial declared.

"This facility must be disabled. I will get you a written order from the president confirming that this facility poses a danger to national security and must be destroyed. The president has already stated that if the facility holds what we think it holds it should be disabled."

"Wait," Matt said. "You say disabled, but don't you mean destroyed?" "I mean making the facility unusable, sealing it up," Mr. Six answered. "I'm a bomb specialist. I have made three special heat radium bombs that

you will plant in the facility." "Us?" Tangie asked.

"Yes, you," Mr. Six answered.

"You can still get into the facility. I will give you the bombs that you will hide inside flower pots. The bombs are made of material that won't be detected by the scanners."

"You put those planters around the atrium on your last day there. You set the timers at their fifteen minute setting. Then you pull the evacuation alarms, and get the hell out of there. The bombs cannot be shut off once the timers are turned on. They will explode instantly if they are touched again after the timers start."

"Won't such an explosion be heard and possibly damage Carlsbad Caverns?" Tangie asked.

"No," Mr. Six answered. "They are thermal radium bombs with a napalm element. They are heat generators. The explosions will be rather small. The bombs will flare up instead of a big explosion. The heat will melt down the atrium and all of the entrances, and seal this facility."

"It will take decades for anyone to discover the contents of those chambers," Mr. Dial chimed in. "Maybe then the world will be prepared for the technology they find. The NSA will make the area a designated off-limits property to visitors, explorers, news media, and everyone for a long time." "This is how the president wants to handle this situation. He doesn't like the fact that the CIA is keeping him out of the loop of everything that is going on there. He's been advised not to try to visit the complex because that would make the facility known, and there could be an assassination

attempt on him if he tried to go there."

"But first before all of that, you make sure you have all of your work copied and saved before you shut down and disable that system you have been working on."

"Take this." He handed Matt a small device that looked like a small bulb with a flat metal bottom. It was about the size of a computer thumb drive.

"Attach this to the monitor you are working on. It will record all of your work. That little bulb on the key will blink red for a few seconds when it is targeting in on the data. Then it will turn green when it records the data. Then the green light will go off when it has recorded all of the data."

CHAPTER

37

MEETING IN COLUMBIA

Mr. Dunn's airplane landed at the Bogota, Columbia airport. He debarked and walked through customs and out of the airport with his briefcase and handbag. A chauffeur waited on him outside the airport.

"Hello, Mister Dunn," the chauffeur called as Mr. Dunn approached him and shook his hand.

"Good afternoon," Mr. Dunn answered with a return handshake.

The chauffeur opened the door and let Mr. Dunn enter the back of the limousine.

"I know where you're going," the chauffeur said, as he drove away from the airport. "How was your flight?"

"The flight was fine, but I noticed right away how humid it is here."
"Yes, the humidity is pretty high," the chauffeur responded. "The

closer to the equator the higher the humidity for most countries."
"Especially for me," Mr. Dunn returned. "I don't live in a humid part

of the United States."

"I know you are an important American official here for a very important meeting," the chauffeur continued. "That's all I know, and that's all I need to know."

Thirty-five minutes later, the limousine arrived at a building outside of Bogota.

"See you after your meeting," the chauffeur called as Mr. Dunn exited the limousine.

"I'm counting on it," Mr. Dunn said. He then closed the door and walked to the building.

Mr. Fernando opened the door and greeted Mr. Dunn.

"Mr. Dunn!" Mr. Fernando exclaimed, as he reached out to shake Mr.

Dunn's hand. "Great to finally meet you."

"Same here," Mr. Dunn agreed as he returned the handshake. "I ad- mire your work, and I admire your ability to live in this high humidity." "I'd rather be in a hot climate any day than a cold climate," Mr.

Fernando responded. "Come with me to my office."

They entered Mr. Fernando's office. He sat down in his big office chair behind a huge office desk.

"Nice building and nice office," Mr. Dunn said, as he looked around the room.

"There's good money in Columbia. But our venture will take Columbia to another level."

"In a few minutes my personal assistant and two other officials will be here to pick us up. We will take you on a personal tour of the blighted areas where we plan to build affordable houses, shopping centers, schools, banks, and hospitals. We will go by the places where we plan resorts, golf courses, and amusement parks."

"We will then have a nice meal at the best restaurant in town. We will treat you to Bandeja Paise, Columbia's unofficial national dish. And we will have some other native dishes to go with it."

Later that evening, the envoy arrived back at Mr. Fernando's complex.

The limousine was waiting for him.

"This has been a very educational and pleasurable trip," Mr. Dunn said to Mr. Fernando and his group, as he shook their hands.

"Your chauffeur will now take you to your hotel for a very relaxing evening before you catch your plane home in the morning," Mr. Fernando said to Mr. Dunn, as the driver pulled up to them.

"You will find some company waiting to entertain you in your room," he said with a wink.

"That will be a nice way to top off my visit," Mr. Dunn answered with a smile.

The next morning, Mr. Dunn walked out of the hotel to the limousine waiting for him.

"Good morning, sir," the chauffeur called, as he opened the door for him.

"Good morning," Mr. Dunn returned, as he walked to the car. "How was your short trip?" the chauffeur asked, as they drove away. "Couldn't have gone better."

"Well, just sit back and enjoy a relaxing trip to the airport."

The chauffeur stopped at a light just a couple of miles from the airport. A motorcyclist pulled up and stopped at the light next to the limousine. The person on the motorcycle pulled a pistol out of his jacket and aimed at Mr. Dunn. He pulled the trigger. The bullet pierced through the window and struck Mr. Dunn in his temple. He fell over dead.

The limousine driver pulled the car over to the side of the road. He got out and hopped on the motorcycle with the motorcycle driver. They sped off.

A tow truck pulled up in front of the limousine. Two men got out and hooked up the car. They took the limousine to a nearby automobile wrecking yard. An industrial forklift picked up the car and put it in a car compactor. The hydraulic pistons pushed the crusher down. The crusher crushed the car down to less than a quarter of its original size. The forklift then brought another car and put on top of the limousine, and crushed it.

Mr. Fernando received a call.

"Job completed," the voice on the phone said to Mr. Fernando. "Good. Well done," Mr. Fernando responded. "I am planning a celebration party at my estate for everyone who helped pull off this operation, and for everyone involved in all of our operations."

He clicked his phone off. It immediately rang again. "Hello," he answered.

"Mr. Fernando, I have some disappointing news," the voice on the other end said.

"What is it?"

"I'm afraid the kidnappers you sent to abduct the Americans have been killed," the voice answered.

"What!" Mr. Fernando yelled. "How did that happen?"

"Not sure," the voice answered. "They were in a freaky accident where their car ran off the road on a mountain and exploded, killing all three of them."

"Damn!" Mr. Fernando screamed. Then he calmed down.

"Send another team. This time hire an elite team that will get the job done. And tell them if they can't bring them alive, then bring me their brains. If they left their house, and are on the move, I believe I know how to pull them out of hiding."

"I'm still going to plan our celebration of getting rid of Mr. Dunn and positioning ourselves for taking over the United States of America. This is a huge accomplishment, making the God facility a one-man operation. We will have another celebration when we capture those two gifted scientists." "I'll hire another team that has never failed a mission. They have made me a lot of money over the years."

CHAPTER

38

ABDUCTION KIDNAPPERS AGAIN

Tangie's phone rang, as she and Matt sat in the safe house. She saw on the phone ID the call came from Flo's phone.

"Hello, Flo," Tangie answered her phone.

"Your friend Flo is a little tied up right now." the man answered through Flo's phone, in a Spanish accent. Two other men held Flo with her hands tied and tape over her mouth. They were in an abandoned warehouse near Deming, New Mexico.

"What's going on with Flo?" Tangie asked, and Matt stood up and approached to listen. Tangie turned on the phone speaker.

"We have your friend Flo," the man said. "We don't need Flo. We need you two. Here's the deal. You come to us, and we release Flo."

"Is Flo okay?" Matt asked.

The man motioned for the other two men to remove the tape over Flo's mouth so she could speak.

"Here's your friend," the man said, and held the phone up to Flo's mouth. "Hey Flo, are you okay?" Tangie asked, as tears started rolling down her face.

"I'm okay," Flo answered, in a distressed voice.

"Flo, I'm so sorry for this." Tangie said in a teary voice. "Don't worry," Flo answered. "I'll be fine."

The second kidnapper put the tape back over Flo's mouth.

"Meet us in the old mining town Shakespeare, New Mexico in four hours. Come unarmed. Turn yourselves over to us and we release Flo."

The man clicked the phone off.

"Oh my God. They kidnapped Flo!" Tangie yelled in tears. "And it's all our fault. Her life is in danger because of us."

"It's terrible that such a bad thing has happened to such a sweet person," Matt said. "They may have sinister plans for us, but I pray they let her go."

"Yes, pray," Tangie agreed.

The man who had talked to Tangie and Matt threw the phone on the warehouse floor and stepped on it, crushing the phone. He then turned to Flo, who was being held on both sides by the other two men.

"Well," the man said as he looked Flo up and down, "we have a couple of hours before we need to leave. How about some fun with this nice black cougar."

He pulled out a knife, and waived it in Flo's face. She turned her face away from him. He slipped the knife under her dress and bra strap at her shoulder. He cut the garments and the straps fell, exposing her left breast. The other two men piled up some old papers behind her. The first man pushed her backward, onto the papers. She screamed under the tape.

• • •

"All I can think of is Flo," Tangie said, as they drove toward Shakespeare. "We are in danger, and I don't know how things will turn out with us, but I pray Flo gets through this."

"Yes," Matt responded. "This really brings home just how big this whole thing is. All the way from the president to an innocent orphanage owner. With weapons that can destroy masses of people. I know you are praying, just pray a little harder."

Three hours later, the couple arrived in Shakespeare. They drove up the old dusty main street until they saw a van. One man stood outside the van, holding his handgun.

The couple stopped about one hundred yards from the van and got out of the car.

"My precious cargo," The man called to them. "Where's Flo? Let her go!" Tangie called.

The man looked at his van and waved his hand. The other two men stepped out and pulled Flo out. Her hands were cuffed with plastic cuffs. "Hold your hands in the air and walk forward away from your car,"

the man called, pointing his gun at them. They walked about ten yards from their car and stopped.

The man nodded his head to the other men. They cut the cuffs from Flo's hands.

"Goodbye lovely," the leader said, as he pushed her toward Matt and Tangie. Flo held her dress and bra strap at her shoulder with one hand as she walked briskly toward the couple.

"We're so sorry!" Tangie said to Flo, as she embraced Flo. "It's all our fault" Matt said as he also hugged Flo.

"Don't blame yourselves," Flo said as she hugged them. "I'm okay. God is good. I will be praying for you."

Matt handed Flo the keys to their car.

"Get them and tie their hands behind their backs, and put the blinders over their eyes, and put them in the van. Get their phones and destroy them first." The two men did as the leader commanded.

An hour later, they arrived at a house that sat alone near the New Mexico border with Mexico.

"Take them upstairs," the man commanded as they pulled the couple out of the van.

Once upstairs, the men sat the couple in chairs, and took their blinders off.

"Allow me to introduce us," the man said, as he stood over them waiving his 9-millimeter Glock. All three men held their Glocks.

"I am Manuel. This is Tipoley." He pointed to the kidnapper on his left. Then he pointed to the other kidnapper on his right.

"This is Dennis. Imagine a Hispanic named Dennis."

"We weren't told much about you, just that you are a very valuable mujer and hombre. The people who hired us to abduct you paid us three times our usual rate."

"So do you know them?" Matt asked, hoping the men will continue providing information.

"We just take orders. We are professional abductors. I prefer to use the word abductors. Kidnappers sounds so amateur, like those amateurs who got themselves killed trying to abduct you."

"We are pros. We do this for a living. Abducting Americans for drug cartels and foreign governments is our most profitable venture."

"So can you tell us where we are going?" Tangie asked.

"All I can tell you is that our mission is to smuggle you into Mexico, where we will deliver you and receive the second half or our abduction payment. What happens to you after that, we don't know."

"We will stay here overnight, and travel in the morning."

"Tipoley, take them separately to use the bathroom. When you get back Dennis will go get us all something to eat. I'm going downstairs to transmit some data."

"You two will have to sleep in your chairs. It's not my job to keep you comfortable, just to deliver you."

Tipoley secured the couple back in their chairs after he took them to use the toilet. Dennis left to go get food.

Tipoley sat in a chair facing the couple with his gun pointed at them. "Don't ask me anything," he said to them. "I don't have any answers

for you." Tipoley then lit a cigarette and sat back.

The three of them sat there for about thirty minutes in silence, while Manuel was downstairs transmitting on a desktop computer.

Tangie addressed Tipoley. "You know, this is not a Godly thing you are doing."

"Stop talking about this God of yours or I'll put tape over your mouth." Tipoley angrily responded.

Matt spoke to Tipoley.

"Hey man, how about lighting me up a cigarette before you go to the toilet?"

"You don't look like the smoking type," Tipoley responded.

"You do things you might not ordinarily do when you're nervous and unsure about your situation. I know nicotine relaxes the brain."

"You can't even smoke," Tipoley responded. "I'm not untying your hands."

"I'll wing it and do the best I can," Matt answered. "Don't deny a man his dying wish."

"Okay," Tipoley answered. I'll give you your dying wish."

Tipoley looked down the stairs intending to tell Manuel what he was doing, but decided not to since Manuel was still busy on the computer.

He pulled out a cigarette, lit it, and put it in Matt's mouth.

"Don't go anywhere," Tipoley said then let out a chuckle. "Don't think you can get very far with a chair strapped to your backs." He left the room. Matt leaned over behind Tangie's chair and held the lit cigarette against the plastic tie around her hands. After a few seconds, the hot cigarette melted the tie enough for Tangie to break it. She then grabbed the

cigarette and held it to the plastic tie around her ankles.

"How did you know he had to use the restroom?" she asked as she held the very short remaining cigarette against Matt's tie around his wrist then his ankles.

"The power of suggestion," Matt answered. "He had not yet used the restroom since we arrived."

"Now how do we get out of here?" she asked. "There's no door up here, and the only window has bars on it."

"Now it's kill or be killed," he answered." That's the only way to get out of here."

"Doesn't your Bible say there's a time to kill? I don't think that means just killing animals for food and clothing. I think it also means you have to do what you have to do to protect and save yourself."

When Tipoley came back through the door. He looked at the empty chairs. Tangie came from behind the door and jumped on his back and wrapped the plastic tie around his neck. He dropped his gun. Matt came around to his front and punched him hard in his stomach. He fell to the floor with Tangie hanging on tightly.

Matt grabbed his hands while Tangie continued strangling him with the plastic tie. He struggled for a few more minutes, then went still.

"We have a gun now," Matt whispered. "This gives us a chance against the other two." They dragged Tipoley's body over to the corner from the door.

At the same time Dennis arrived with the food.

"Take the food up there and see what's going on," Manuel said to Dennis. "Sounds like Tipoley may be trying to entertain our abductees. He loves to dance."

Dennis walked up the stairs and entered the room. Matt jumped from behind the door and put a chokehold on him. He dropped the food. Matt wrestled him to the floor and laid him on the floor on his back. Tangie stuck her fingers behind Dennis' trachea. He froze stiff, then went limp.

"One more to go," Matt said, as he and Tangie stood up.

"Not so fast?" Manuel said, as he stood in the doorway pointing his gun at them.

"Hands up and back away from those guns!" he ordered. They backed up with their hands in the air.

"Seems you two are smarter than most people," he looked down at the plastic cuffs.

"Melted the plastic cuffs with a cigarette? Never seen that trick before. I always thought the ties were more efficient than metal handcuffs, but you showed me a flaw in that assumption."

"I could use you two on my team now that you took out my men, if there wasn't other plans for you. I've only lost one man in all my fifteen years of this abduction business, so this is a very unfortunate day for me." "But all is not lost. I still have my abductees, and now I get my partners' shares of the reward. And the kicker is my orders were if I can't bring you there alive then just your brains will do. And since my help just checked out on me, I don't have any choice but to lighten my load and just

take your thinking caps to the people who want you."

He raised his gun. At the same time a bullet smashed through the window and bars and struck him in his chest. He fell dead instantly.

Matt and Tangie slowly walked to the window and looked out. They saw a man approaching carrying a long-range rifle.

As he walked closer, they recognized him.

"It's Mr. Six," Tangie called. They hurried down the stairs and out of the house to meet him.

He walked up to them.

"You've been tracking us," Matt surmised.

"It's a good thing I was." Mr. Six answered. "Or you might not be here to express such great appreciation for having your lives saved."

"How did you keep track of us?' Tangie asked. "Those abductors smashed our phones in Shakespeare."

"Technology." Mr. Six answered. "When your phones got smashed by those abductors, they sent off an automatic signal to follow anyone who had touched the phone by their fingerprint biometric signals for up to three hundred miles and six hours. I had your signal and the bad guys' signal who touched your phones. We call it the dog sniffer signal, because it's like a dog being able to find things based on its scent."

"The only issue is that the signal is not real time. It is fifteen seconds behind."

"If it was twenty seconds behind, we wouldn't be here," Matt concluded. "You are probably right." Mr. Six said.

"I have two firebombs in my car." Let's blow these bastards and their van to bits then get out of here. My car is just over the hill. I need to get you two back to work to finish the job."

"First take us to Flo," Tangie ordered. "We owe her a lot."

CHAPTER

39

DEA ABDUCTION

"Flo is such a wonderful person," Tangie stated as she and Matt drove away from the orphanage. "She is so forgiving."

"Yes," Matt added. "She could have been psychologically scarred for life from the way she was brutalized by those abductors. Not to mention not wanting to have anything to do with us again. But she is moving on like nothing happened to her."

"It's not surprising," Tangie retorted. "She is such a strong loving Christian woman. She was tested, and passed the test with flying colors. She could have cut us out and everything related to her terrible experience. And I would have understood if she wanted to leave all of that in her past. But still I am extremely thankful that she welcomed us back. I don't want to ever lose our relationship with her."

"If there is a heaven, they will roll out the red carpet for her," Matt concluded.

"If?" Tangie asked. "With all we've been through you don't think God had a heavy hand in saving us?"

"I'm still sorting things out. You can say we got lucky, or were blessed, to survive alien and human abductions. But you can also look at it that we have been in danger, and experienced a lot of terrible things you wouldn't wish on your worst enemies."

"We lost our home. We're losing our jobs. I don't know if all the work we have done will be useful, or used in the right way. I think I can say we were at the wrong place at the wrong time."

"You can also technically say we could have been at the right place at the right time too," Tangie responded.

"I know our lives are not settled right now. Things have taken a turn. But we are also tested, and need to pass the test just like Flo did. The Bible speaks of hope and patience, and not letting things trouble your heart."

"You mean you don't have any stress or negative thoughts about the things we are going through?" Matt asked.

"I didn't say I don't have anxiety and concerns. You have to also know that the Bible says we will have trials and tribulations. But God can take any negative situation and turn it into a positive thing that can change your life, and can have a great effect on others' lives. We have testimonies that can help other people."

"You forget we can't talk about a lot of what we do," Matt quipped. "I think we can find ways to dress it up," she responded.

"You mean lie?" he asked.

"No, not lie. Just say what happened in fairly generic terms."

"I can testify that we were abducted by some very bad people, and God saved us. There's a way to say things that can still have a positive effect on people."

"Maybe," Matt agreed. "But I'm still fighting with the subject of alien abductions. I don't know if I want to elaborate on those experiences."

"You say what you feel like saying," she responded. "And you keep in what you don't want to share with anyone. Just look at it as we love each other, and went through everything together. So, we know what we both experienced. And that's all that matters as far as sharing with other people."

"I agree with that," Matt concluded.

"You know," Tangie said, "I'm looking forward to the day we are settled again. I'm looking forward to going back to church in person, rather than streaming."

"There's a lot to look forward to, including getting to know Jamie, as well as the other kids."

"Yes," Matt added. "We have made good progress with Jamie. He actually interacted with us this time."

"And you know," Tangie added. "I've been thinking about what Jamie said to me about someone taking his father."

"What do you deduce from it?"

"He could be talking about an alien abduction. Flo has been looking into missing person's reports in New Mexico. Nobody matches what would probably be his dad."

"He's had a traumatic experience. He could have a traumatic experience from just anybody taking his father, but I get the feeling something else was involved, that it was a little more than just people abducting his father and him running away."

"Maybe his father was somebody special if it was an alien abduction," Matt added.

"Maybe so. There are many accounts of missing people who are never heard from again. It's possible he will never see his father again."

In the next moment, a black sports utility vehicle passed their car and started slowing down in front of them. Matt looked to pass the vehicle, but another black SUV pulled up beside their vehicle. Another black vehicle pulled up close behind them.

"What's going on?" Tangie called, as all three vehicles started slowing down, causing them to slow down.

"I don't know! But they have us surrounded!"

The front passenger window of the SUV beside them rolled down. An arm stretched out and pointed to the side of the road for them to pull over on the shoulder of the road. All vehicles pulled over.

Three men from each of the three vehicles jumped out with their hand guns drawn on the couple's vehicle. They immediately held up their hands.

"They're going to kill us!" Tangie yelled.

"I'm not sure!" Matt returned. "They look like they are from the Drug Enforcement Agency," he said, as they could see the men had DEA jackets on.

All of the men took a couple of steps toward Matt and Tangie. Then they stopped with their pistols still up and pointed at the couple.

"What do they want with us?" Tangie whispered.

"I don't know," Matt answered. "But we don't have any drugs with us." "They can always plant some drugs if they really want us," she retorted. Matt looked in his rear-view mirror.

"There's a man getting out of the car behind us," he said. "Looks like he doesn't have a gun. He must be the head of whatever they are planning to do. I feel another abduction coming. They are called abductions when somebody or something wants to take you against your will."

The man walked up to Matt's window, and motioned for Matt to roll down his window. Matt did as commanded. The man took off his dark glasses.

"Matt and Tangie Riley," he stated with a slight grin. "Nice to meet you two scientists, geniuses, warriors, and escape artists. You can put your hands down. We're not gonna shoot. We're the good guys."

They lowered their arms, and exhaled a breath of relief. All of the agents put away their weapons.

"I'm special agent western field commander George Rhodes. Don't be surprised that I know your names. Unlike the CIA, we work closely with the NSA on all things American."

"What do you want with us?" Matt asked.

"I'll fill you in when we get off this road. We want you to go with us on what I will call a journey for now. Follow us to the next town, where we will put your vehicle in storage for a few days."

A half hour later, Officer Rhodes closed down the door of the storage unit where Matt and Tangie had just driven their car into.

"Come with me," Agent Rhodes commanded, and he walked to the driver's side of one of the vehicles his men had driven to the storage facility. "I'll see you men in two days," he said to his men, while he waved them

off, and they loaded into the two other vehicles. Matt and Tangie got into the vehicle with agent Rhodes.

"So, where are we going?" Tangie asked agent Rhodes, as they drove away from the storage building.

"I'll tell you when we get there," the agent answered. "I will reveal some things to you right before they happen. That makes it more dramatic, and that's just the way I want it. Plus, I want to see if you two discover what we're doing before I tell you."

"This sounds like somebody else we know," Tangie responded.

"You wouldn't be talking about the infamous Mr. Six, would you?" the agent asked.

"I should have known if you know us you would know Mr. Six," Matt surmised.

"Yes," Agent Rhodes answered. "Known and worked with him for a while. But the NSA works with him more. And I know what the NSA and Mr. Six's plans are for the God facility. That's one of the reasons why I have you here now."

"Why?" Matt asked. "Do you plan to stop him?"

"Absolutely not," The agent answered. "We're supporting the plan as much as we can from a distance."

"You used the term infamous," Tangie said.

"Yes," Agent Rhodes answered. "Mr. Six works outside the lines a lot. That's why the NSA won't put him directly on their payroll. He does a great deal of dirty work for them. And he's a brilliant performer. We call him Unibomber Two because of his knowledge and skill at making various kinds of bombs for specific purposes."

"I'm taking you back to Albuquerque. We're going to visit two places. I would call them places that should put things into proper perspective for you."

"And I gather we're not going to know what those places are until we get there?" Tangie asked.

"That's correct," Agent Rhodes answered. "You can look at it as a type of game. But this is no game."

"Since you had a plan to take us places, why did your men have those guns drawn on us?" Tangie asked.

"You two are skilled with weapons and hand to hand combat," Mr. Rhodes answered. "It was more for protection of my men than a threat to harm either of you. I had never met you, so I wasn't sure how you would react."

CHAPTER

40

THE ALBUQUERQUE VISIT

About an hour after they left the town where Matt and Tangie put their car in storage, they arrived with Commander Rhodes in downtown Albuquerque. He parked in front of one of the high-rise buildings. "Let's go inside," Agent Rhodes commanded. He flashed his badge at the security guards as they entered the building, and then led them to the elevator. He pushed the button for the tenth floor. They didn't say a word to each other as they entered and rode up the elevator, all anticipating what would happen when they reached their destination.

The elevator stopped at the tenth floor, and they stepped out.

"This was America First Bank." Mr. Rhodes exclaimed, as they looked at the scrapped off print of the bank's name on the glass doors of the office facing the elevator.

"Let me guess," Matt spoke up. "This is the bank that handled our paychecks."

"Correct," Agent Rhodes answered. "But it's a little more involved than that. But you're one for one with your assessment of your journey so far."

"There's nothing here," Tangie added, while they looked around at an empty office. "I gather this was a crooked bank that the financial regulators closed."

"You're half correct," Mr. Rhodes answered. "Follow me."

They walked past the teller station and broken ATM machine and down the hall. At the end of the hall was a large room. The only thing in the room was flip chart on a stand. The first page on the chart had a map of the country of Columbia.

"This was a crooked bank," Mr. Rhodes answered. "But the financial regulators didn't close it because it was not a chartered federally insured bank. The regulators found out about it and let the FBI know. The FBI and the NSA closed the bank."

He then walked up to the chart and picked up a pointer that was lying on the shelf of the chart.

"Almost all of the cocaine used in the United States comes from Columbia," he stated, while he pointed to a map of the South American country. "Hell, almost all of the cocaine used on planet earth comes from Columbia."

"Most of the coca plants are grown and cocaine produced in this Andean region and Catatumbo region, and also the southwestern provinces like Nariño, Cauca and Putumayo." He pointed to those regions on the map.

"The main cartels that controlled the drug business were the Medellín, Cali, Norte del Valle, and North Coast cartels. The Medellin cartel is by far the biggest drug cartel in Columbia. I'm sure you know about the two powerful drug lords in Columbia that were finally caught; Pablo Escobar, known as El Chapo, and Dairo Antonio Úsuga, better known as Otoniel. You probably know a lot of this. What you may not have known is how it ties to your paychecks."

"Let me get to where you come in. Cocaine and other drugs are shipped illegally into America by land, air, and sea. The powerful drug cartels hide their profits by flushing them through the vast global financial market, using various methods including internet payment plat- forms, cryptocurrencies, payment cards and real estate. Then, they use the laundered cash to underwrite their trafficking. We believe a member of the Columbia Defense Ministry, a man named Carlos Fernando, made arrangements and permission for the drug money to go to the cartels, as well as his personal account."

He flipped the page on the chart. The next page had a map of the United States. Most of the larger cities in the western states had lines leading to Albuquerque on the map.

"The drug pushers in all of these cities gave their ill-gotten funds to the drug runners who brought or wired funds to this so-called bank."

"Which the CIA knew about and ran?" Matt questioned.

"Correct," Mr. Rhodes answered. "Or should we say the CIA set up to track drug money."

"Which they used to pay us?" Tangie asked.

"Not just to pay you, but for a number of things. Mainly those other projects on lever four where they worked with alien crafts and their contents to reverse engineer the items in that chamber."

"This bank had a special account with State Bank, where you had your accounts. Some of the money was sent from this America First Bank to State Bank to pay you and a few other legal entities. America First also wired money to the drug cartel accounts in Columbia. The funds were washed when America First would withdraw funds from State Bank. State Bank never questioned the legality of their transactions, or if America First was a legally chartered bank."

"The bank was not legally chartered, so it did not have to file a currency and foreign transaction reports for cash transactions over ten thou- sand dollars. They are called CTRs, and that's how our government keeps up with large cash transactions. Without those reports, it's hard to trace large cash transactions and transfers."

"But the federal regulators did eventually find out, I presume?" Matt asked.

"Yes," Mr. Rhodes answered. "They found the account, and started asking questions about it. State Bank couldn't come up with satisfactory answers. So that's when the regulators contacted the FBI."

"A man named Bill Moyer ran America First Bank and the shell company America First. America First had a legal charter as a corporation, but was the front for the bank," he explained, as he flipped the page to the next chart, which had drawings of the bank, connected by lines to those banks, and the banks in Columbia.

"The NSA abducted Mr. Moyer while the FBI and financial regulators were closing in on him."

"What happened to him?" Tangie asked.

"That's classified information," Mr. Rhodes answered. "It's even classified to me. But I have a feeling he's spilling his guts about the inner-workings of the bank and Level Four, or he may be just spilling his guts if he isn't providing information."

"But the point I'm making here is that you were paid with drug money.

The CIA did not give you the full picture when you were hired."

"If they had," Tangie countered. "We wouldn't have taken the jobs. Although Proverbs Thirteen Twenty-Two says the wealth of the sinner is laid up for the righteous."

"I want to take you to the next leg of our journey," Mr. Rhodes said, while he threw down the pointer and closed the pages of the flip chart.

Twenty minutes later they pulled up and stopped at the Albuquerque Addiction Treatment Specialist Center. There was a line of patients seeking treatment that stretched two blocks.

"Look at that line of drug addicts," Mr. Rhodes said while he pointed to the people queued up. "This is the original source of your paychecks. Let's get out."

Mr. Rhodes led them to the people in front of the clinic. There was about fifty people in line.

"Hey!" Mr. Rhodes yelled to the crowd. "Raise your hands if you lost your jobs because of your drug addiction?" About two thirds of the people in line raised their hands.

"How many of you lost loved ones due to your drug habit?" About half of the line raised their hands.

"I lost my job, my wife, my kids, my home, my money, my dog, and all of my friends," one man in the line in tattered clothes yelled out. "I'm homeless."

"Let's go inside," Mr. Rhodes commanded, as Tangie started walking toward the man.

"You still have Jesus," she called, as they walked away and toward the door of the clinic.

"If so, I wish he would help me with my drug addiction!" the man yelled back.

"He will today!" Tangie responded. They walked into the clinic.

"I'm here to see your director, Ms. Euvanda," Mr. Rhodes said to the receptionist. "I'm Agent George Rhodes with the DEA."

"Okay," the receptionist answered. Then she pushed a button on the pad on her desk and relayed the message.

"It's a sad scene to see that line out there," Matt said to Mr. Rhodes, while they waited for the clinic director.

"What's even sadder is that there will be a line of totally different people out there tomorrow," Mr. Rhodes answered.

After a couple of minutes, the clinic director emerged from the side door.

"Hey George," she called as she reached out to shake Mr. Rhodes hand. "Gloria, it's good to see you again," he responded, as he returned her

handshake.

"These are my two assistance, Matt and Tangie Riley." They shook her hand as they were introduced.

"Come to my office," she called, as she walked to the door she came out of and opened it for them.

"I want you to give them a quick education on the drug problem, specifically drugs from Columbia, that effects Albuquerque and New Mexico alone," Mr. Rhodes said. "They will be able to relate the local area statistics to all of America."

"Sure," she responded, as she opened her office door, and they all entered her office.

"Let me start with a staggering statistic that more than seventy five percent of deaths in Albuquerque are from illegal drugs."

"Wow!" Tangie said. "We are not blind to the drug problem in America, but that stat is unbelievable."

"Let me give you some more facts," Ms. Euvanda said. "They paint and even more sobering picture of drugs, and what Columbia alone is responsible for."

"You see that picture over there?" she said as she pointed to a picture on the wall of a woman, and they turned their heads and looked at the picture. "Her name is Judy Bonner. She died of a cocaine overdose at the age

of thirty. She was the director of this clinic before I came here. You see the picture of the little girl beside her? That's her four-year-old daughter Sage. She also died of a drug overdose. Let's go over some more hard facts."

About an hour later, the three of them got back into Mr. Rhode's vehicle.

"Was any of what you saw and heard today disconcerting?" Mr. Rhodes asked the couple, as they entered the vehicle.

"Not only disconcerting," Tangie answered, "but unreal, sobering, and sad."

"We're planning a big cocaine and gun bust the day after tomorrow," Mr. Rhodes said. "It's the result of a yearlong investigation of the Columbian Mexican drugs for guns exchange between the two countries. I want you two to be there as observers."

"We'll stay here in Albuquerque tonight and tomorrow night. Thursday morning, we will drive to southern California.

CHAPTER

41

DEA COLUMBIAN/MEXICAN OPERATION

On Thursday morning, Matt and Tangie prepared to leave their room at the hotel in Albuquerque where they had stayed for two nights.

"Another unknown operation," Matt stated, as he opened the door for Tangie to exit before him.

"God has a plan," she returned.

Mr. Rhodes waited for them in the hotel lobby.

"Good morning," Mr. Rhodes greeted the couple. "Good morning," they returned.

"Let's drive," Mr. Rhodes said as they walked out of the hotel and entered his SUV. "We have about a twelve-hour drive. So, get comfortable. We'll grab breakfast and a later meal on the way."

"We went over part of the Columbian drug and money connection to the United States the other day. The Columbians also trade drugs for weapons for protecting their drug trade. They get the weapons from Mexico.

Mexico gets the weapons from China. They purchase them cheap with their own drug profits."

"Our undercover operation tells us that a large drug for weapons trade is taking place tonight in Mexico at a drug cartel landing port. It will be the largest drug and gun bust in US history. About twenty tons of cocaine will be brought in by two narco submarines from Columbia, and traded for so many AK forty-sevens and other guns that they will bring another submarine to help the other two carry the guns back to Columbia. Guns weigh more than cocaine. They will use two narco subs to carry up the drugs, but need three subs to carry back the weapons."

"Are you going to Mexico?" Matt asked. "Or are you going to wait to seize the drugs as they try to get them into America?

"The American DEA has special permission to enter Mexican waters and Mexican territory to seize both the cocaine and the guns," Mr. Rhodes answered.

"We have a team of eight well-trained and well-armed agents who will be waiting on us at a Coast Guard port in southern California. We will also have two snipers going with us who will position themselves in areas around their secret port who will cover us as we move in to make the bust. We will also have a news reporter from San Diego embedded, who will be there to tape and report the arrests and seizure."

"I just want you to be with us on the Coast Guard cutter. Not on land in Mexico. Since you have been getting paid from this drug arrangement, I wanted you to see part of how we put a dent in their operations. We will destroy their secret port, and blow up the narco subs. This will be a huge signal that we are stepping up our war on drugs. It also means we may be looking to compete with the NSA for your services, and we want you to see what we do."

"How do you know how much firepower they will have to resist you?" Tangie asked.

"We have an informant with them," Mr. Rhodes answered. "He infiltrated their ranks almost a year ago. He has their trust. He will be providing information to us through a sophisticated communication ring he has been wearing since the undercover operation started. It beams to a secret satellite that we will have positioned directly over the zone. I can talk to him every five minutes if I want to."

"We will have good communications and good firepower, but we expect to surround them and make the seizure without a firefight. If we have to fire, we will have a drop on them. We have night vision goggles, so we should see them before they see us. Our informant will tell us if they have night vision goggles. We have night vision blocking scopes if they try to see us."

"We'll go as you wish," Tangie said. "But I don't feel great about it." "You mean about you going or the mission? We are fully prepared,"

Mr. Rhodes responded. "If I were in your shoes, I would feel the same way. But I'm in my shoes. We've trained for almost a year for this. It's time to roll."

Later at dusk, the three of them arrived at a Coast Guard port on the southern California coast. They exited the vehicle, as they watched Mr. Rhodes' agents in fatigues load the Coast Guard rapid cutter with weapons and support equipment.

As they walked to the cutter, Mr. Rhodes started yelling instructions to his men. Tangie looked at the boat. The name on the boat was Devil's Lair. "Why is the name of the boat Devil's Lair?" Tangie called to

Mr. Rhodes.

"They named it that because they like to think it goes to places where there's danger." Mr. Rhodes answered.

"After this mission I think you should rename it," Tangie said. "Why not name it John Three Sixteen?"

"For God so loved the world, that he gave his only begotten Son, that whosoever believe in him should not perish, but have everlasting life."

"The captain named it," Mr. Rhodes answered. "We're just using it for this mission."

"Still, Mr. Rhodes," Tangie responded. "I still have that bad feeling about this mission."

"Nothing can be changed," Mr. Rhodes answered. "This is the perfect time to pull off this mission. Calling off this mission is above your and my pay grades. Besides, how can things go badly with a boat you want to rename John Three Sixteen?"

Another vehicle pulled up, and a women got out of the vehicle with recording devices. Mr. Rhodes stopped.

"Welcome Cathy!" Mr. Rhodes called to her. She walked up and shook his hand.

"It's good to see you again, George." she said as she reached out to shake his hand.

"Cathy," he said. "Let me introduce you to Matt and Tangie Riley, soon to be former CIA operatives who will be going with us."

"Matt and Tangie, meet Cathy Zang, of KSD News in San Diego." "Nice to meet you two," she said, as she shook their hands."

"Nice to meet you, Ms. Zang," they both said as they returned the hand shake.

"Please, call me Cat," she said. "And it's great to meet you two. I know about you and the things you have done. You are heroes in my eye. But don't worry about me telling anything. I work for an office of KSD that only covers secret operations. I don't make any of my work public without permission from the top. The top is usually the American government. And I don't have and don't expect to publicly report any information about you." "Let's get on board," Mr. Rhodes commanded. "They have fatigues waiting for us below deck to change into. This is combat, so we all might

as well look like it."

"You look so handsome in military fatigues," Tangie said to Matt, as they finished changing into the green and grey combat fatigues in a cabin below the deck. They embraced in a kiss. "You look so military. Like you're ready to march and fight."

"You look pretty good yourself," he responded. "I like you in green. You're sexy, in a military way. I wouldn't want to fight you. You look sexy but tough."

"Compliments will get you everywhere," she responded, and they kissed again. "Let's go up on deck and catch the wind and listen to the waves in the night air."

"You go ahead," he answered. "I want to take a quick nap before Mr.

Rhodes briefs us again in an hour."

"Okay, I'll go up, but I have to say I don't feel good about this whole thing. I wish they would call it off."

"You heard what Mr. Rhodes said," Matt responded. "Changing things is above our pay grades. And I get the feeling he really wants to do this not only for himself, but for his country."

"I guess you're right. I'll see you later."

She walked up the stairs to the deck of the rapid cutter. She saw Cat on the deck's stern side taking videos of the coast, and also of her surroundings. She saw Tangie walking toward her.

"You come up to catch the wind and sea air?" Cat asked. "Yeah," Tangie answered.

"Please join me," Cat said, as she stopped taking videos. They both leaned out over the rails facing the ocean.

"I'm capturing as much of this as I can," Cat said, feeling like she had to tell Tangie what she was doing. "I want the entire story of this operation from start to finish. To be part of a huge drug bust on foreign soil is gigantic. I'm not looking for publicity or promotion. I just want the big story. And this bust may take fighting the war on drugs to another level."

"I hope so," Tangie added. "By the way, your last name is Zang?" "Yes, I'm Chinese. And here's my story. I used to be an undercover

reporter for Communist China. I did basically the same thing I'm doing now, except sort of in reverse. I reported on the Chinese citizen's plans for uprisings and plots against the Chinese government. I reported to the Chinese government, not to the people."

"So did that keep you busy?"

"Pretty busy. But I didn't like the punishment the government would do to the people when I reported on them. They would be jailed, tortured, or killed. When I spoke up about it, the government made arrangements for me to come to America to report on American citizen's and the American government plots and plans against China. I decided to defect to America. I knew some American reporters who helped me get my job at KSD. And low and behold, I'm still reporting on secret stuff."

"Like you and your husband, we're good at what we do. So, people keep asking me to do this secret stuff. I actually said I wouldn't leave American soil again, but I'm not going that far."

"I have to tell you," Tangie said. "I haven't felt great about this mission from the start. But knowing what I'm learning about you, it seems you're as gung-ho about this mission as Mr. Rhodes."

"Yeah. I'm glad to be a part of it, and I'm actually not afraid, with all I've experienced."

"Okay," Tangie said "Since this mission is a go, let's talk about other things. So, do you find a lot of secret things in San Diego?"

"More than you would think."

"With the large naval base there, something is always going on. There are more plots and plans to attack or invade the base than you would think.

As a secret reporter, I get access to top secret information, and to surveillance equipment."

"Being such a large naval base with high tech aircraft and weapons and stuff, do you see a lot of spying and strange aircraft in the area?" Tangie asked.

"You mean UFOs, don't you?" Cat asked. "Yes. Both spying and UFOs."

"I've seen some really strange things. UFO's are known for hanging around military bases. Since we are both sworn to secrecy, I'll show you some really strange UFOs that I have on video that I don't want you to share. And believe me, there are some things the American military has no clue what they are. They are so sophisticated that they make us look less than cavemen."

"I'll share some videos with you after this mission. And speaking of secrets and high technology, I believe one of our former presidents slipped and said that he's seen some things the American military has that China and Russia does not know about. I don't know about Russia, but China has some things that America does not know about, and that I am sworn to secrecy about. They have some things reporters are not allowed to see."

"If you know so much wouldn't China be after you?" Tangie asked. "I don't think so. It's called Eyes Wide Shut. The American government advised me not to change my name, believing the Chinese would be looking for someone who had changed their name. Plus, my job is secret. Not many people know that some networks have a secret reporter. When we make this bust, my video will go public at some point, but I won't. And besides, if I die, I rather die for America than China. I helped them do some awful things."

"Don't talk about dying," Tangie said. "Let's talk about living. The Bible speaks of always looking to the future."

"I don't know much about your Bible," Cat responded. "Well, I can teach you. I love talking about Jesus."

"Maybe we'll do some of that on the way back," Cat said.

"By the way, I know you're planning to destroy the GOD facility in New Mexico."

"You know about that? How did you find out? I thought that was highly classified."

"I have sources in Washington. Our president can't keep secrets. Anytime the president knows something, other people know. That's why the CIA keeps them out of the loop on many things."

"I would actually love to see those technologies being developed come to manifestation in our lifetime, but others think differently. Now it will be fifty to a hundred years or more in the future before the world gets to benefit from those technologies."

"Or harmed by those weapons," Tangie retorted.

"I'm glad to see you believe in your cause," Cat returned. "That means you will be successful."

"I wouldn't say it was my cause. I have slightly different objectives about my career."

"Well, ladies, how's the midnight air treating you?" Matt asked, as he popped up from below deck.

"It's good for the circulation," Cat answered.

At the same time, Mr. Rhodes approached from the cargo hold. "We'll be at our anchoring point shortly," Mr. Rhodes informed

the three.

"There we will air up our four inflatables, and paddle to our point two clicks above their base. Boats with motors would have made too much noise, so we're paddling to shore."

"It's time for me to check in with our informant." He held up a small microphone.

"Hello Jimmie. How's it going?"

"Going well," Jimmie answered. "It's a little cramped on this sub, so I have to whisper. We have three subs, two packed with coke. About six men will be coming ashore. I would say we're about thirty minutes out.

"Okay Jimmie," Mr. Rhodes answered. "I'll check back with you when you're ashore to find out how many men are on shore and what kind of weapons they have."

"We're getting ready to anchor. We're about a mile off shore. The men are coming up in a minute to inflate our boats. The helmsman, your boat driver, will remain here with you Matt and Tangie. At the front of this boat in that floor locker are two fully loaded M-sixteens just in case you need to use them for any reason. Hopefully you won't need them for anything, but they are there."

The eight agents and two snipers ran up the stairs and started preparing the boats to launch. After the ship anchored, they put the boats in the water. They handed arms, equipment, and paddles to the first men to get on the boats. They strapped their night vision goggles to their heads. Mr. Rhodes held up a map and went over it with the pilots of the inflatable boats. He then helped Cat into the boat. She had her video equipment strung around her neck."

"See you in a few," she said to Matt and Tangie. "Be careful," Tangie called back.

"Be safe," Matt said. "All of y'all, be safe!"

"I'll see y'all on the other side," Mr. Rhodes said to Matt, Tangie, and the boat driver, as he was the last to get on the boat. He boarded, then offered a salute to the three. They saluted back. Then the four boats paddled off out of sight.

"Ever shot an M-Sixteen?" Tangie asked Matt.

"It's no different from the other automatic weapons we've shot many times," Matt answered. "It's just the military's version."

They looked at the helmsman.

"Don't look at me to fire a gun!" the boat driver exclaimed. "Besides, they only left two for you two."

"So that means you know how to fire a gun?" Tangie asked with a grin. "I don't know weapons," he answered. "I just know how to drive

the boat."

Fifteen minutes later, the DEA agents and Cat landed and tied up their boats on the Mexican shore. Mr. Rhodes pulled out his talkie to make contact with Jimmie, their informant.

"Come in, Jimmie," Mr. Rhodes called. "Come in, Jimmie," he called again. Again, no answer. He called Jimmie three more times.

"Can't reach our informant right now. Maybe the satellite is not in place right now."

"What do you do now?" Cat asked.

"We move as we planned," he answered. "We're gonna assume there's probably five to ten men at their dock, including truck drivers. Let's move with caution. Put your night goggles on."

"What's that light up there in the sky?" the helmsman asked as he pointed up to the sky to the southwest.

"I don't know," Matt answered. "Looks like it's not moving. Maybe it's the communication satellite Mr. Rhodes is using to communicate with his informant."

"It seems low for a satellite." Tangie said. "I know it could be higher than it looks. It's probably the satellite, since Mr. Rhodes said their communication satellite would be directly above them, and that's the direction they were heading."

Then they saw a flash of light in that direction. "Did y'all see that flash?" the helmsman asked.

"Maybe that was a flash of lightning," Tangie responded.

"I checked the weather carefully before we sailed," the helmsman responded. There was no bad weather forecasted for tonight. The mission would have been cancelled if we were going to have weather issues."

Gunshots started going off on the ground in that area.

"There's gun shots!" Matt shouted. "There's a firefight going on!" "Oh God!" Tangie called as she put her hands up to her face.

"I hope our guys are winning the fight!" the boat operator called. "Lots of shooting!" Matt called, as they looked at the gun flashes in

the far distance. Then they saw several fire explosions. "Look at those explosions!" the boat driver yelled. "I don't like the looks of this!" Tangie called out. After a few more minutes, the firing stopped.

"It's silence," the boat operator called out. "I wonder what that means." "How will we know?" Tangie asked. "Do you have communications

with them?"

"No!" he answered. "Agent Rhodes wanted radio silence with the boat to protect us."

They were quiet for a few minutes. Then they heard a sound in the water. "I hear splashing in the water!" Matt called, as they looked in that

direction.

"That's paddling!" The boat operator called, as they looked toward the sound.

After a minute, they could see one of the DEA agents paddling his boat toward them. He yelled at them.

"What's he saying?" Matt called.

"I don't know yet!" the other two answered. As he got closer, they could understand him.

"Pull the anchor! Start the boat!" he yelled. "Pull the anchor! Start the boat!"

"He said pull the anchor and start the boat!" the boat driver called.

And he ran to do what the agent screamed for him to do.

"Come on!" Tangie yelled, as they could see the agent was in serious distress.

He paddled up to the boat, and they pulled him in.

"Let's get out of here!" he called to the boat driver, and the driver frantically pulled in the anchor and started the engine.

"What happened?" Tangie asked, as the agent breathed hard.

"We got ambushed!" the agent called, as he gasped for breath. "Get us out! They were coming after me!"

The driver revved the engines and pulled the throttle full bore. "Mayday! Mayday!" the helmsman called over the boat talkie. "Where is everybody else?" Matt asked.

"They're all dead!" he yelled. "Oh God!" Tangie gasped. "What happened?" Matt asked.

"We lost communication with our inside informant Jimmie at drop- off. So, we walked one click to our separation point. We tried to hear from him again. Again, no answer."

"As we gathered to go over our plans, this flash of light came down on us. We were blinded for a few seconds."

"When the light left and we could see again, we looked around for George, and we didn't see him anywhere. He just vanished."

"Then, lights turned on from our front and side. We could see men in front of us. One of them held up Jimmie's head. They had cut his head off his body. The man yelled, 'Is this the snitch you are trying to talk to?'

"Then they opened fire on us. We scattered and tried to return fire. I made it back to our boats and started paddling. Everybody else is killed or captured!"

"Oh my God!" Tangie yelled, and started crying.

"I believe they're coming after us!" the agent said, after several gasps. Then they heard the sound of boat motors. Two engine powered air boats were following them and closing fast.

"That's them!" Matt yelled.

Shots started coming from the boats, and hit the back of the cutter. "Get down!" Matt yelled.

The shots kept coming as the boats drew closer. One shot hit the boat driver in the back. He fell down, and the boat slowed down. They looked at the driver falling and back at the two boats approaching.

"I'll drive!" the agent jumped up and ran to the boat controls. The boat sped up again.

"Stay down!" Matt yelled to Tangie. He crawled on the deck to the locker with the guns. He reached up and pulled out the two M-16s. He slid on the deck back to where Tangie laid.

"Let's return fire," he yelled to Tangie, as he handed one of the loaded M-16s to her. Bullets whizzed above them.

A couple of bullets hit one of the cutter's engines. Gas started spewing out. The boat slowed down some.

Matt and Tangie raised up and returned fire and quickly ducked back down.

"Look at the splash of the water!" the agent yelled to them, as he operated the boat. The boat driver squirmed on the deck holding his shoulder where he was shot.

"What?" Matt yelled back.

"Look at the white waves the boats are making in the front. Those sound like air boats. Aim and shoot at the waves and you should hit the boats and puncture them!"

"Put pressure on it!" he yelled down to the boat operator.

Matt rose up and spotted the waves of the first boat and started firing at the waves. The bullets hit the air boat and punctured the tube. It immediately slowed down and started sinking. He ducked back down. The men in the boat jumped off with their life jackets.

Tangie quickly rose up and fired at the front waves of the second boat.

It too started sinking.

The firing stopped. They and the agent breathed a sigh of relief. "Let's keep going!" Matt yelled to the agent.

Tangie looked back at the water. She could hear the men scrambling around in the water. She looked up in the sky and saw a light far be- hind them.

"I still see that light we saw earlier!" Tangie yelled. "I think it's following us!"

The agent looked back and saw the light. He picked up the talkie. "Mayday! Mayday!" he yelled. "This is CC Devil's Lair! Send help per

Operation Glow as pre-determined!"

"Repeat! This is CC Devil's Lair! Send help per Operation Glow as per-determined!"

"This was our Plan B if things went badly," the agent yelled out to Matt and Tangie.

A voice came on the talkie.

"Copy that, Devil's Lair!" the voice called. Matt and Tangie could hear the voice.

"We are scrambling as per pre-determined Operation Glow! I see your location on radar."

At Marine Corps Air Station Miramar, California, an alarm went off at Hangar 1. Four men scrambled toward two F-35B fighter jets in the hanger. Within two minutes the fighter jets were in the air headed toward the boat.

"That light is gaining on us!" Tangie yelled. The engine that had been hit by the bullets puckered out. The boat slowed down even more.

"Let's start shooting at it when it gets within range!" Matt commanded. "I only have a couple of rounds left!" Tangie called to Matt.

"I have maybe four!" Matt called back. "I'll go see if there is any more ammo in the locker." He walked up and opened the locker.

"No more ammo!" he yelled back to Tangie, and he slammed the locker door.

"I don't think a few rounds are going to be enough to bring that thing down!" the agent called, as he tried to get the boat to go faster.

"It's all we got!" Matt called back.

"It's coming!" Tangie yelled, as she and Matt stood and took aim at the approaching orb.

At that minute, they could hear the engines of the approaching Navy fighter jets. They looked to the north and saw the jet lights coming to- ward them.

When the jets reached them, the orb shot up and disappeared into the night sky. The jets flew over the boat.

"This is Pilot Rick Philpot!" a voice came over the boat speaker. "A Coast Guard cruiser is headed your way."

The smugglers in the water held on to their punctured boats and life-jackets, and started firing their guns at the boat.

"The smugglers in the water are firing at us!" the agent radioed to the jet pilots. "Can you take them out?"

"Roger that!" the pilot radioed back. The jets turned around and headed back toward the boat.

The pilots flew in low, and located the smugglers in the water. They strafed the water with their machine guns, and left a bloody trail in the dark water.

Then the jets turned and headed toward the smugglers exchange port.

The smugglers saw the jets approaching, and scattered into the woods.

The jets fired four AIM-120 missiles at the port. The truck that had the weapons exploded. The missiles sank the three submarines.

Matt and Tangie looked at the explosions light up the night sky off in the distance.

"Plan B should have been Plan A," Tangie spoke. "We would have twelve Americans still alive."

"Yeah," Matt responded.

They looked at each other. They then headed to the injured boat driver to help him.

"There's a first aid kit down below in the galley," the agent called to them.

42

RUSSIAN RESPONSE

"What do you think went so horribly wrong with the mission?" Matt asked Mr. Dial on a speaker phone, while he and Tangie sat on board a CIA chartered flight back to Albuquerque. "And where is Mr. Six today?"

"That's what we are investigating," Mr. Dial answered from his Washington D.C. office. "And Mr. Six had to go on a short undercover assignment. I don't keep up with everything his organization does."

"Twelve people killed or missing, including the informant and a news reporter." Tangie said somberly. "I'm praying for their families."

"Mr. Dial," Matt called. "Several questions come to my mind about the failed operation."

"First, who do you think informed the smugglers that the DEA was planning the bust? Do you think the informant turned coat? He was with the cartel people a long time."

"I can only speculate at this point," Mr. Dial answered. "Like I said, our investigation is just beginning. My gut tells me that he was loyal to America. George Rhodes knew Jimmie real well. They went to high school and college together. If Jimmie showed any signs that he had started working for the other side, I believe George would have picked up on it." "Your next question is probably about George Rhodes himself. I know

he disappeared during the firefight. It looks awfully suspicious. I don't know if the smugglers took him when the men experienced the blinding light. An asset as valuable as George could be a good bargaining chip for them."

"Speaking of that light," Matt said, "that bright orb was in the sky above the rendezvous area. And it looked like that flash of light came from what looked like a craft. What are your findings so far on that? Could that orb have interfered with the satellite communications, causing Mr. Rhodes to lose contact with his informant? And could whoever or whatever was in that spacecraft have been working with the smugglers, since it was coming after us? I don't think it was coming with any friendly intentions toward us." "I have no answers at this time," Mr. Dial answered. "Our investigation is just beginning. The fighter pilots didn't see the object."

"But from what I know, most aliens are working with the United States, not against America. At least that's the case of what I know from the Bill Moyer abduction."

"What else do you know about aliens?" Tangie asked. "That's all I can share right now," he answered.

"And I'm wondering if the Chinese were involved in the operation," Tangie said.

"They were supplying the arms for money. And I suspect they still wanted to take care of Ms. Zang. And they could have been the ones who informed the cartels about the DEA plans."

"I believe we will know at some point," Mr. Dial concluded. "In the meantime, you two need to get back with Mr. Six and get back on track for your operation at the God facility."

"I'm sure we'll hear from him when he wants to hear from us." Tangie said. "He has a curious sense of timing. I'm sure wherever he is today it's where he wanted to be."

• • •

In Moscow, Mr. Volenski sat in his office and talked to three other Russian officials.

"Damn it!" he yelled out in Russian, as he pounded his fist on his table and stood up.

"We were on the verge of something big before Mr. Dunn disappeared! We were about to abduct the United States and hold them hostage to our desires. Now we got to start all over with American abduction plan!"

"Mr. Dunn was our best spy," one of the other men in the room spoke. "He moved up the ranks of the American spy system. He provided us a lot of information. He will be very difficult to replace."

"This is a huge setback," another officer in the office said. "We may never catch up with the United States in anything in our lifetimes. We lost our chance to abduct America!"

A KGB agent knocked on his door. "Come in," Mr. Volenski called out.

The agent opened the door and walked up to the front of Mr. Volenski's desk.

"Mister Volenski," the agent called in Russian, and offered a salute. "It took us a few weeks, but we have now found out what happened to

your American mole Mr. Dunn. This is the result of a joint operation with Interpol, and with the American National Security Agency."

"We found out the Columbians murdered Mr. Dunn."

"Our response will be swift and deadly!" Mr. Volenski yelled.

Three nights later, Mr. Fernando hosted a celebration party at his large compound outside Bogota, Columbia. A Columbian official ranged the doorbell. Mr. Fernando answered the door.

"Officer Felasco," Mr. Fernando called. "Welcome to our celebration of big things to come for our country."

"Happy to be here," Mr. Felasco answered.

"I haven't been here in a while. I almost forgot that your palace is as large as any drug cartel kingpin's estate. Good thing you greeted me. I may not have found you."

They both laughed.

"Come on in," Mr. Fernando called. "There's about thirty people here.

We have a cumbia band playing in the main lobby."

"We'll get something to eat, drink some Aguardiente and rum, and then talk a little business. And I want to introduce you to Sangia, the lady who entertained Mr. Dunn on his last night to be alive. Maybe she will entertain you before the night is over."

"We also will toast those men who took care of those American agents and their reporter who was trying to disrupt our arms and drug operations with Mexico. They thought they were going to disrupt our network and slow us down. But we showed them how capable we are, and embarrassed the American law enforcement agencies."

"We lost a few men in the operation, but the others who escaped the American attack are here. Shipments in the future will make that one look like a drop in the bucket."

About an hour later, Mr. Fernando, Mr. Felasco, two officials, and a drug cartel kingpin gathered in Mr. Fernando's large office.

"I want to show you the map of how we will divide up and control the United States," Mr. Fernando stated, as he rolled out a map of America. The map had the United States divided into six sections.

"From America, we will control the world. Before we discuss the American territory, let's toast to our venture and upcoming success. The Americans are too smart for their own good. But they don't know an American abduction is taking place. We need to abduct America before China buys it all up. They are doing their own American abduction."

They all raised their glasses and clanged them together.

About 10,000 miles up in the Earth's orbit, a Russian satellite beamed in on the Fernando complex. Outside in the night ski, a drone recorded Mr. Fernando and his visitors' conversations while they talked and toasted in the room. The drone also had a camera that focused in on Mr. Fernando and his men.

Off the coast of Central America, deep in the Pacific Ocean, aboard the Russian nuclear-powered submarine Venskopie, a Russian officer sat and listened to Mr. Fernando's conversations, while he also looked at a screen of the Fernando complex.

"We have him," the officer called over to his commanding officer. The commander leaned over and viewed the monitor. The commander looked over to his petty officer.

"Fire at will!" the commander yelled.

The petty officer motioned to the skipper, who called co-ordinances out to the two gunners.

The gunners repeated the co-ordinances. The first gunner flipped three switches. The second gunner flipped two switches.

On the topside of the submarine, a hatch opened, and a cruise missile shot out of the silo and up through the water.

When the missile left the water, its rocket fired, and it shot up into the night sky.

Ten minutes later, the missile slammed into Mr. Fernando's villa. The explosion leveled the place, and killed everyone there.

"We got him!" the officer said to the captain, with a thumbs up motion, as he looked at his monitor of the burning rubble of Mr. Fernando's compound.

"Good," the commander stated. "Let's go home."

43

FINAL VISIT TO G.O.D. COMPLEX

"I know it's been a while since I've seen you, Mom," Tangie said on her new phone to her mother, as she and Matt rode to the GOD facility. "I know you had top secret work," Mrs. Turner stated, "but I didn't think it would keep you this tied up. We haven't seen y'all in months. You couldn't even make it home for Christmas."

"Mom, I promise you'll be seeing us very soon. We have one last mission, then we will have some time off. We're changing jobs to something that will allow us more time to visit."

"Okay," Mrs. Turner replied. "I hope to see both of you soon. Tell Matt I said hi."

"Okay, Mom. Love you."

"Love you, baby. Take care." Mrs. Turner said.

"Okay, Mom. Goodbye." Tangie ended the conversation, and clicked off her phone.

The two entered the atrium of the GOD facility. Tangie carried one of the flower pot bombs. Matt carried the other two. They placed the pots against the walls of the atrium rectangular fashion equal distance from each other. They then entered Level Two.

They sat side by side at the programmer screen. Matt took the recording device Mr. Six gave him and attached it to the modem computer. The device started blinking red for a few seconds. Then the red turned to a solid green. After a few minutes, the green light went off.

"Let's get out of here." Matt said, as he removed the recording device from the modem and put it in his pocket.

They went to the atrium and pulled the flowers from over the bombs, and flipped the switches on the bombs. The digital numbers started counting down from fifteen minutes.

They walked over to the wall and pulled the emergency switches. Red lights started flashing all around the atrium. A siren started going off. A voice bellowed out, "Emergency! Please exit the facility!" The voice repeated over and over.

"Let's go!" Matt commanded. They ran to the elevator. He pushed the button. Nothing happened. He pushed the button several more times. "The elevator's not working!" he yelled. "It must automatically turn

off during an emergency situation!"

The repeating voice then said, "Please evacuate the facility! Do not use the elevator! Please use the stairs!"

"Where are the stairs?" Tangie yelled.

"I don't know!" Matt answered "The whole time we worked here I never knew anything about any stairs that came down here!"

They looked around the atrium, but saw no indication of stairs. "Let's try our Level Two lab!" They ran to the Level Two door and

opened the door using Matt's finger ID on the scanner. They ran in and looked around the lab. They walked quickly around and pushed buttons and wall panels and drawers.

"There's no stairway in here," Tangie yelled. "Let's see if we can get into Level One!"

They ran out of Level Two and to the Level One door. They tried to use their finger ID on the scanner, but nothing happened.

"Nothing's happening!" she yelled.

They looked around the atrium. The bomb timers were down to nine minutes.

They ran to the elevator again.

"Let's try to pull open the doors!" Matt said. "Maybe if we can get in, we can open the top of the elevator and climb up the shaft."

They positioned themselves on each side of the elevator doors and put their fingers in the crack of the door and pulled in each of their direction. But the door didn't move.

"It's no use!" Matt called. "Let's see if we can put in the correct code to get into Level Four."

They ran to the Level Four door. Matt frantically pushed the numbers on the key pad. Nothing happened.

"We've got six minutes!" Tangie called when she ran over and looked at the timer counting down on one of the bombs.

"I wonder if it was Mister Sixes plan to blow us up with this facility!" she called.

"If it was, looks like he's pulling it off!" Matt answered.

All of a sudden, the Level Three door opened. They looked over at the door, as the timers counted down to four minutes.

A small robot about two feet high rolled out. Lights flashed on the top of the robot.

"Everyone, evacuate now!" the robotic voiced called as it rolled around the atrium. "Use the Level Three stairs!" It repeated.

The two ran through the open Level Three door and to the stairwell door. They opened the door and ran up the stairs.

"So, Level Three is just a stairway!" Matt called, as they ran up the stairs. "Let's move. We probably only have less than a minute."

"And we don't know how far we need to climb. We never knew how far down the facility was."

A few seconds later the first bomb exploded. Then the second bomb exploded. A few seconds later the third bomb exploded. The explosions made the stairs move and shake. The couple lost their balance when the stairs rocked. They gathered themselves and continued running up the stairs.

They looked down and saw fire coming up the stairs. "Faster!" Matt called.

They finally reached the top of the stairs and opened the door to a cave tunnel, as the fire approached. They closed the door back and ran. The fire melted the door, and the tunnel started to collapse.

The tunnel roof collapsed behind them as they ran through the tunnel. The lights in the tunnel went off behind them as the cave tunnel collapsed. Inside Carlsbad Caverns, the ground started to shake. Some of the stalactites and stalagmites started to move. Visitors to the park looked

around and grabbed rails.

Some of the stalactites broke free and fell to the ground.

"It's an earthquake!" a visitor yelled, and the visitors ran out of the cavern exits.

Matt and Tangie ran through the twists and turns of the tunnel until they came to two men standing at the door exit to the caverns.

"Where do you think you're going?" one of the men called to the couple. "The complex is caving in!" Matt yelled. "We're just trying to get out of here."

"We have strict orders not to let you leave the property," the second man stated.

"What are you talking about?" Tangie called. "The place has blown up. We all need to get out of here!"

"We have your photos," the first man said again. "We know who you are. We are ordered not to let you leave this exit if you tried. That would be a sign that you are deserting the complex. We can't let that happen."

The men started to draw their guns. Tangie ran up to one of the men and kicked him back. He flew back into the door. His gun fell away from him. Matt simultaneously ran up to the second man and grabbed his hand holding the gun. The gun fired up in the air several times until all the rounds were fired. Matt punched him in the stomach. He bent over. Matt then hit him with an uppercut, and he fell backward.

The first man bounced off the door and ran toward Tangie. She grabbed him by the chest and rolled over backward and slammed him flat on his back. She turned to him with her fists ready for him, as he also assumed a fighting position.

The second man ran low to Matt and grabbed him around his waist, and the both of them fell to the ground. The man jumped on top of Matt and started to hit him in his face. The first swing knocked Matt's head sideways.

Matt blocked his second swing and third swings. Matt reached up and grabbed the man's neck, and rolled him off of him.

The cave-in approached the fighting foursome. The fighting continued. Both sides traded blows, missed swings, and kicks.

The first man took a final swing at Tangie. She ducked. She kicked her leg at him. He ducked her kick and knocked her back. He started toward his gun and she jumped on his back. He backed up against the cave wall and pinned her. She yelled as he slammed her against the wall, and let him go. He turned around and started to hit her. She ducked the swing, backed up, and kicked him in the groin. He yelled and bent over and grabbed his crotch. She then jumped and twisted and kicked him hard in his head. He fell backward and his head slammed against the ground, and knocked him out.

At the same time, Matt held on to the man around his neck as the man tried to swing at him. Tangie picked up one of the guns, came up from behind the man, and hit him in the back of his head with the pistol handle. The man stammered back from Matt's chokehold. Matt came up to him, turned, and elbowed him to the head. The man stammered backward

and hit the back of his head against the tunnel wall and fell out.

The couple looked at the cave-in walls approaching.

"Let's go!" Matt yelled. Tangie looked down at the men. "Let's drag them through the door and run."

They drug the two men outside and into the cavern away from the door. They closed the door and ran. The cave-in blew the door open. The sign on the outside of the door that read "Authorized Personnel Only" flew through the air.

"Those bombs were a little more powerful than we thought," Tangie said, as she and Matt ran out of the cavern with the other park visitors.

"Are you okay?" Matt asked Tangie, while they stopped outside the caverns to catch their breaths.

"I'll be okay," Tangie answered. "I'll feel these bruises for a couple days.

I would say this time those men knew how to fight."

CHAPTER

44

CIA ABDUCTION OPERATION

"I gather you have the key with all of the information?" Mr. Six asked the couple on speaker phone, while they relaxed in the lobby room of the safe house.

"Yes, we do," Matt answered. "Those were quite some bombs." "Yeah," Mr. Six answered. "Those bombs were one of a kind. We weren't totally sure how the bombs would react that far down in a tight space. We went on a ninety seven percent chance the bombs would per- form as expected according to our field tests. And when I say 'we,' I mean myself and the NSA."

"We got the collateral damage covered. The media put out a message that there was a small earthquake near Carlsbad Caverns. The national park service also assured people that the park is open and safe for visiting again." "You have that covered," Tangie said, "but we were almost covered ourselves. We barely escaped."

"Let's both take a little blame for that," Mr. Six retorted. "The bombs were a tad ambitious, but you two are responsible for knowing how to get out of your workplace. How did you think the people that worked in Lever Four got in and out? You never saw them. They used the Level Three entrance, which had a stairway and elevator with another entrance to Level Four."

"That wasn't your average workplace," Matt responded. "It's a secret facility, and probably not a lot was known even by the people working there. It took a robot to help people out."

"Speaking of exit escapes," Mr. Six said, "every place should have an escape route. We need to talk."

Outside the perimeter of the safe house, a black Chevrolet suburban pulled up and stopped. Five men and one woman in military style uniforms exited the van carrying M-4 assault rifles.

They gathered together. The leader addressed the group.

"Tim and Toby," he ordered, as he pointed to the two men. "You two come in from the northwest perimeter."

"John, you and Sandy take the southeast perimeter. Jay and I will come to the front from this side. Put your packs on, and let's roll."

"Yes, sir," they all answered.

The security cameras in the safe house went blank. Moments later, the electricity went off. All of them put on their night vision goggles, and approached the house with their guns drawn.

"Jay, fire!" the leader commanded. Jay shot tear gas grenades through a front window. John shot tear gas grenades through the back window.

The two last men threw ropes up to the roof and scaled up to the second floor, where they shot tear gas grenades throw the window.

All of them put on their gas masks.

The leader and his companion kicked open the front door, and slowly walked in with their guns drawn.

At the same time, the two in the back kicked open the back door and entered.

The two men upstairs entered the house through the second-floor window.

All of the agents walked carefully through the house looking for its inhabitants.

"You seem to be very good at giving us information at the last minute!" Matt called to Mr. Six on his phone while he and Tangie ran through the tunnel away from the safe house.

"Your safe house wasn't so safe. Was that the CIA after us?" "Yes, it was," Mr. Six answered. Settle down and let's talk." The two stopped to take a breath some ways down the tunnel.

"We should have known the CIA would come after the people who blew up their complex. They won't stop until they find us."

"Well," Mr. Six said, "there's good news and there's bad news regarding the CIA."

"What is it?' Tangie asked. "And give us the bad news first."

"The bad news is that those six agents probably will hunt you until they find you," Mr. Six said.

"How do you know how many there are?" Matt asked.

"Frank Stenner, and his five henchmen, with one being a woman," Mr. Six answered.

"He runs the off the books program of the CIA that managed the GOD facility. Destroying that facility has set off a wave of repercussions. And I'm afraid much of the repercussions involve taking care of you two." "All five of his accomplices have collectively murdered over two dozen innocent people. The woman, Sandy Alamar, butchered her entire family.

That psycho slaughtered her husband and her two young daughters with a butcher knife."

"The CIA took them off death row and gave them new identities to do a lot of dirty work, which of course, they agreed to do."

"Why didn't they just shoot a missile or something and just blow up the safe house?" Tangie asked.

"They probably wanted you alive, and probably want the key you have," Mr. Six answered.

"Why don't you tell us the stuff we need to know before we need to know it?" Tangie screamed into Matt's speaker.

"Maybe I've been around your government agencies too long," Mr. Six answered. "The timing of providing information is usually on a need-to-know basis."

"That's not good enough when our lives are at stake," Tangie responded. "Anyway," Mr. Six continued, "I have a fix on the staging area where Stenner and his team are staying. We have to turn the tables on them and

take them out."

"We?" Matt asked.

"Yes, 'we,'" Mr. Six answered. "You two and me."

"The NSA won't get directly involved with this task. It's a long and complicated process when it comes to taking on other government agents. They will be gone by the time anybody else would plan to go after them. And with the facility destroyed, I just don't see that happening."

"You don't work for the NSA yet, so they are only going to do so much to protect you."

"Instead, they now look at you as government contractors, doing off the book work for them."

"On top of that, you two know how to shoot and how to fight. They probably couldn't get better people to do the job, especially this fast."

"And it's your lives you are protecting. It's kill or be killed. If this doesn't happen, their search for you will turn from abduction to elimination. And they won't stop. Their only mission now is to eliminate you."

"What do we have to do?" Matt asked.

"I intercepted their communications. Their staging area is a seedy motel outside of Flagstaff. It's at the end of a shopping complex. They are leaving the day after tomorrow. We need to get to them before they leave and scatter, and regroup later."

"I know you have guns and ammo. I'll bring the explosives. You can pick me up at our meeting place in Tucson, and we'll go over our plan on the way."

"What's the good news?" Tangie asked. "Could there possibly be any good news about all of this?"

"The good news," Mr. Six answered, "is that Stenner's clandestine program is top secret. The CIA does not even acknowledge that he or his program exist. That gives him freedom to do what he wants. But if he is eliminated, he never existed as far as the CIA is concerned. So, no one else will be looking for you after these people are taken care of."

"See you tomorrow evening."

"I can't believe this!" Tangie said, as she exhaled a heavy breath while Matt clicked off his phone.

"G I Joe and G I Jane, against our own government." "Kill or be killed," Matt responded.

"Getting a little tired of that," Tangie said. "We're not killers."

"I think we show that practically everyone has the capacity to kill, given the right circumstances," he returned.

"That circumstance being kill or be killed. We need to get back to the safe house to get the EV. That's where our weapons and ammo are."

"Let's hope they didn't take it," she added.

"If they did, they get more than just guns," Matt added. "Mister Stenner knows about that power piston. If he gets that, he will have salvaged something from his operation. No telling what he will do with it." "And we're not giving Mr. Six or Mr. Dial the information they want from us on that key until everything else is taken care of, and we are safe."

45

REVERSE ABDUCTION OPERATION

"Plans have changed," Mr. Six said to Matt and Tangie the next evening, as he threw a backpack and duffle bag into the back seat of their SUV. He hopped in and turned on his computer wrist watch.

He leaned forward and stretched his hand out between the two.

"Some more of your last-minute information," Tangie said, as she shook her head.

"This time it wasn't my decision," Mr. Six said. Mr. Dial's face came up on the watch.

"Good evening, all," Mr. Dial said. "There's been a slight change to your mission."

"Instead of taking out all six agents, the powers that be want Frank Stenner taken alive. Your jobs just became a little harder."

"Why do they want such a dangerous man to remain alive?" Matt asked.

"Frank oversaw the whole God facility for the CIA. He was Bill Moyer's boss. Although the facility is now sealed, he has valuable information some important people want about what was in that complex. They are specifically interested in Level Four. They believe alien technology was used to develop the devices in Level Four. They believe there were companies waiting to patent and use those devices. They also want to know what and how the CIA planned to use those things. They don't believe all those devices were intended for peaceful applications."

"What do you plan to do with him after they get that information, or if he refuses to talk?" Matt asked.

"That's classified information," Mr. Dial answered.

"I suspect whatever happened to Bill Moyer will be the same fate for Frank. You won't have to worry about him turning up alive anywhere."

"I'll see you all after the mission." Mr. Dial signed off. "How do we plan to capture him?" Matt asked.

"I have a tranquilizer dart gun," Mr. Six answered. "We just need to get a shot at him. He should fall instantly no matter where the dart hits him."

"Here are pictures of the agents we are after."

He handed the pictures to Tangie, and they looked them over.

"I know you two have photographic memories," Mr. Six said. "And you will recognize these people when you see them."

"The CIA plans for a lot of things, but I bet they didn't plan that you would go on the offensive and go after them," Mr. Six said. "They won't be expecting us to take the fight to them."

"The shopping complex should be empty by the time we get there." "They will plan to regroup, get updated intel, then go after you again

if we don't get them now."

"I have another place we can meet when this is over."

Three hours later, the trio stood on a hill overlooking the motel. They peered down at the buildings through their binoculars. They were all dressed in black. It was about one o'clock in the morning.

"There are other people staying at the motel," Mr. Six said. "Our assault has to be a surgical strike. We have silencers on our pistols. That will help things. But they are probably not staying in consecutive rooms, so the whole building is vulnerable."

"How do we know what rooms they are in?" Tangie asked. "We don't right now," Mr. Six answered. "But we will shortly."

Mr. Six picked up his backpack, which lay on the ground beside them. "I'll be right back," Mr. Six said, as he started walking down toward the two-story motel.

"I wish he wouldn't wait till the last minute to let us in on things," Tangie said.

"Yeah," Matt agreed. "Our lives are on the line. There is an air of mystery about him."

"It's more than just a mystery if you ask me," Tangie responded.

Mr. Six walked into the motel lobby with his backpack. The motel doorbell rang.

A man walked out from the office and to the front desk.

"Can I help you sir?" the man asked, in a Middle Eastern accent. "Yes, you can." Mr. Six answered.

"I work with the National Security Agency." Six said, as he flashed a badge at the man. "Are you the owner of this motel?"

"Yes, I am," the owner answered. "I need your help, Mister???" "Nazihr, sir," the owner answered.

"Look, Mister Nazihr, there are some wanted people staying here, probably under fake IDs. I need to apprehend them. There may be some disturbance to your other residents."

"So, you're saying there could be some damage to my building?" Nazihr asked.

"Look," Mr. Six responded, while he laid the backpack on the desk and unzipped it. The backpack was full of wrapped stacks of one-hundred-dollar bills.

"There's enough cash here for you to build a better motel than this one."

"What do you want me to do?" Mr. Nazihr asked, while he looked down excitedly at the money.

"Here's what I want you to do."

"First, in twenty minutes, I want you to sound the fire alarms and get everyone evacuated from their rooms. Make sure they all gather in this front parking lot."

"Then you disappear for several minutes. Then you return to them and tell them there is no fire and send them back to their rooms."

"Then you go somewhere safe for a couple hours."

"After two hours, turn off the electricity to the building, tell them you have no power, get everyone left checked out of your motel, and send them away. It will be daylight then."

"Then you get far away from the building." "Got it?"

"Got it, sir!" Mr. Nazihr answered, with a smile on his face. "And give me your master key," Mr. Six ordered.

Mr. Six walked back to the perch where Tangie and Matt waited. "What's going on?" Matt asked.

"In a minute there's going to be a fire alarm," Mr. Six answered. "The owner will have everyone evacuate their rooms and gather in the parking lot. Let's move a little closer down to get a good look at them and see what rooms they go back to."

"It would be good if you tell us the plan before you execute it!" Tangie said, in a bit of anger.

"I had to be sure it would work first," Mr. Six answered.

"Then you tell us what you plan to do, and we'll see if it works," Matt responded.

They walked down closer to the motel, still in the dark.

The motel alarms went off. The residents exited their rooms and gathered in the parking lot.

"I see them," Tangie whispered, while they looked at the crowd in the parking lot. "All six of them."

"Me too," Matt added.

The motel owner came out to them and told them there was no fire, and it was a false alarm. He sent the residents back to their rooms.

"There's one of them going into room number five," Mr. Six whispered. "There's two of them entering room thirteen," Matt added.

"There's another one going into room twenty-one," Tangie reported. "Stenner and the woman are going upstairs," Mr. Six noted, as the couple walked to the stairs, then up the stairs. They stopped for a minute

at the top of the stairs and chatted.

A car pulled into the parking lot. Two women got out and walked to and up the stairs.

Mr. Stenner walked to and entered his room on the front of the second floor. The two women walked into the room with him. Mr. Stenner's female partner, Sandy, walked to the back of the building.

"She must have a room on the backside," Mr. Six said.

"I'll get her," Tangie said. She left and walked around the edge of the parking lot and snuck behind a dumpster behind the motel. She pulled out her pistol.

"The hookers with Mr. Stenner kind of complicate things for the one man we need to take alive," Matt said to Mr. Six.

"We still need to get him at all costs," Mr. Six answered. "Let's move!" Tangie did not see which room Sandy entered. She panned the rooms,

while she contemplated her next move.

Then Sandy exited her room and stood on the balcony and lit up a cigarette. She paced back and forth. Tangie tried to get a good site on her moving target.

"Stand still," Tangie whispered, as she pointed her gun toward Sandy. Then Sandy stopped, and leaned on the balcony handrail. Tangie had her in her sights.

"Jesus," Tangie whispered, "I have to give her a fighting chance."

Tangie put her gun back into her pants, and moved toward the motel stairwell. She quietly tiptoed up the stairs. At the top of the stairs, she stood and looked at Sandy puffing her cigarette.

Tangie stepped out. Sandy looked around and spotted her. Her eyes lit up when she recognized Tangie. She turned toward Tangie.

"So," Sandy said in a calm voice, "since we didn't find you, you decided to find us."

"Looks like it," Tangie answered. "Was the plan to capture or kill us?" "My plan was to send you straight to hell!" Sandy answered, in a

mean tone.

"I'm not going to hell," Tangie responded. "Even if I die tonight." "There's no heaven," Sandy answered back. "Only the dark abyss." "Only for unbelievers," Tangie said. "How can you believe in hell but

not believe in heaven?"

"I stopped that line of thinking a long time ago," Sandy answered. "This world is too mean and hypocritical for there to be a reward for any- one here, especially for people like me."

"Well, there is," Tangie answered. "Even for people like you. All you need to do is believe."

"Not a chance!" Sandy yelled. "The only reward I'm looking for is the reward we get after taking care of you and your cohorts."

"I hear you're a pretty good fighter," she said to Tangie, as she flicked her cigarette over the rail.

"Looks like we're about to find out," Tangie answered.

"Yes, indeed!" Sandy called. She then ran at Tangie and grabbed her around her waist. They both fell to the floor. Tangie's gun fell down the stairs. Sandy rolled on top of Tangie.

Sandy swung at Tangie's head four times. Tangie blocked her four swings, but her fifth swing landed and knocked Tangie's head to the side. Tangie coughed. She then rolled Sandy off of her. They both stood up and into fighting positions.

Sandy kicked at Tangie twice. Tangie ducked the kicks. Sandy kicked at Tangie a third time, and Tangie blocked her kick, while continuing to stand in a defensive position. Sandy landed a punch to Tangie's face. Tangie fell back. Then Sandy ran at Tangie, and Tangie grabbed her arm and swung her into the motel wall. Sandy staggered backward, and collected herself.

Sandy landed a kick to Tangie's chest and knocked her back. She then tried to kick two more times, but Tangie ducked the kicks.

On her third kick, Tangie caught Sandy's leg in the air. Tangie swung around and elbowed Sandy in the face and knocked Sandy's head back against the wall. The double hits stunned Sandy, and she staggered back. Tangie then hit Sandy twice in her face. Sandy inched back on each hit. Tangie then jumped and twirled and kicked Sandy in her chest. Sandy fell backward over the banister.

Sandy landed on her head, which crushed her skull. Tangie looked down and covered her mouth as if she didn't want Sandy to dic.

At the same time, Mr. Six and Matt approached room number five. They stood on each side of the door, out of sight of the door peephole with their guns drawn.

"Chances are that even if this master key works, they have their doors locked from the inside," Mr. Six whispered to Matt. "I have an idea."

Mr. Six knocked on the door. "Hey, this is Stenner," Mr. Six said in a different voice. Matt looked at him, amazed at the strange voice.

They heard the inside lock unlock. Mr. Six pushed the door hard and knocked the agent backward. Mr. Six shot the man right between the eyes. He closed the door. He and Matt then slowly walked toward room thirteen.

A man walked out of room nine with a beer in his hand. He looked at Mr. Six and Matt with guns in their hands. Matt put his finger up to his lips to silence the man. Matt pointed him back to his room. The man ran back into his room and closed his door.

When Matt and Mr. Six reached room thirteen, they heard moaning, and the bed screeched inside the room.

"Are you going to use Mr. Stenner's voice again?" Matt asked Mr. Six. "I don't think they'll hear me," Mr. Six answered. "They're too busy

enjoying themselves."

Mr. Six kicked in the door. The two naked men looked up from the bed. Mr. Six shot one agent in the head. Matt shot the other agent in his chest. Both men fell back dead on the bed.

"I really don't like taking people's lives," Matt said, as he closed the door, and addressed Mr. Six.

"It's not a good feeling, no matter if they were going to kill you. But it looks like you are a pro at it, and can sleep at night without even thinking about it."

"You do what you have to do," Mr. Six answered. "In this case, it is kill or be killed, carrying out the death sentences they received but didn't get." "Well, this will be the last time either one of you will have a chance to kill," a voice down the way called out to them. It was the agent from room

21. He had his gun drawn on the two.

"Drop your guns and raise your hands." They did as he commanded. "I now pronounce the death sentence on you."

"Now, where's your third partner?"

"Right behind you," Tangie called, as she stuck her gun barrel to the back of the agent's head.

"Now, you're the one who needs to put your gun down and raise your hands." The agent did as Tangie commanded.

"Now turn around," she commanded.

The agent turned around. Mr. Six picked up his gun and shot the agent three times in his back. He fell dead.

"We could have talked to him," Tangie said.

"The only one who needs to talk is Stenner," Mr. Six answered. "Let's put this one back in his room and go get him."

"He has two prostitutes in his room," Tangie said. "We don't need to hurt them while apprehending Stenner."

"Doesn't matter to me," Mr. Six responded.

"They are people too." Matt said. "We need to make him come out.
I have an idea."

Matt reached down and pulled out the dead agent's cardholder. "This is Agent Jay Grooms. Mr. Six, can you do that change of voice

thing again?"

"Yes," Mr. Six answered

"Okay," Matt responded. "Help me with this guy."

In his room, Mr. Stenner prepared to take off his bathrobe. The two ladies started to get undressed. They had just finished dancing fully clothed, as he had asked them to do.

He heard a knock on his door. He picked up his gun and walked to the door. He motioned the ladies to get back behind the door.

"This is Jay," Mr. Six called in Jay's voice from the other side of the door.

Mr. Stenner looked through his peephole and saw Jay's face.

"Jay, what do you want?" Mr. Stenner asked. "You know I'm very busy right now."

"We found the scientists," Mr. Six responded.

Mr. Stenner put his gun down and opened the door.

Matt grabbed his arm and pulled him out of the door. Matt hit him with a roundhouse punch. He stammered back. Tangie shot him in his side with the tranquilizer gun. He immediately fell to his knees, then fell forward on his face.

Tangie ran into the room.

"Get out of here!" Tangie yelled to the two women. They gathered up their clothes and handbags, and ran to their car.

Mr. Six dragged Jay's body into the room.

"He's heavy," Mr. Six said to Matt. "It wasn't easy holding him up to the door."

"It's time you did your share of the work," Matt answered. "We've been carrying you a lot."

"No time to be a comedian," Mr. Six retorted. "We still got some work to do."

"You need to go get your vehicle and bring me the duffle bag. The duffle bag has incendiary and nitro bombs. I'm gonna burn this place to the ground. The owner will be happy to build a new cheap motel, or ride off into the sunset."

"Let's tie up Stenner. He will be out for six hours. That should be enough time for me to deliver him. I'll take him in his vehicle. I'll meet you two at the new safe house in two days. Mr. Dial will meet us there." "And all of this will be over?" Tangie asked, with an exhausted look on her face.

"It will all be over," Mr. Six answered. "Make sure to bring that key."

EPILOGUE

LAST MEETING WITH MR. DIAL AND MR. SIX

"I still have an uneasy feeling about Mr. Six," Tangie said, as she and Matt drove to meet Mr. Six and Mr. Dial.

"He's saved our lives more than once," Matt retorted. "But I understand your uneasiness. He gives off a single purpose type of persona. And like you, I'm glad we're going to finally be done working with him." "Yeah," Tangie said. "And he's also almost got us killed too. Looks almost like he sets us up. He made the bombs, but we delivered them to the GOD complex. Why couldn't they just have destroyed the complex with a missile?"

"I'm not sure. A missile probably would not have destroyed the complex the way they wanted it destroyed. And it would have had to penetrate a long distance underground."

"I don't think he intended to kill us in that explosion. If we had been killed, he wouldn't get this mind control information. I still believe that is what he really wants."

"I think that's the reason he wanted to use bombs instead of bombing the place. He wanted to make sure we finished our jobs."

"I wish I could feel better about him, Matt. I don't have a great feeling about him down in my spirit. I feel there's a sinister side of him."

"And he was able to change his voice to sound exactly like the CIA agents when we confronted them," Matt said. "He must have been studying them a long time."

"If we take jobs with the NSA," Tangie added. "I hope we don't have to work with him. I can't wait to get this last meeting with him over and done. By the way, how do we handle the issue of the power source of this car? We've put several hundreds of miles on this vehicle, and it still shows a full charge."

"We don't need to do anything," Matt answered. "Mr. Six and Mr. Dial both know about it. Let them take it from here. We don't want any notoriety, fame, or even fortune from it."

"You're right," she added. "We didn't invent it. We'll only accept credit for something we actually develop."

"Speaking of that, we haven't done much mind control work lately.

We've been too busy running and hiding and trying to stay alive." "Yeah. If we go to work for the NSA, it's probably going to feel like we're

starting all over again, rather than using what we have already learned. I kind of feel like we have regressed."

Matt's phone rang.

"Hello Doctor Schinn," Matt answered, after he saw the doctor's name on his Caller ID.

"Hello Matt," the doctor answered. "I wanted to give you an update on the study of that organic chip we removed from your knee."

"What is it?"

"The material didn't match anything in the worldwide DNA bank," the doctor answered. "It was a foreign matter. We wanted to continue studying it, but the strangest thing happened."

"What?" Matt asked.

"We delivered the chip to the testing lab at Los Alamos. When they removed the chip from the container, the power went out in the lab building. When the backup power clicked on, the power in the building came back on, but not the power in the lab room where they were working with the chip. The circuits and outlets in that room had short circuited."

"They decided to wait until the next day while the maintenance crew repaired the circuits and outlets in the lab, so they repacked the chip and put it in storage. The next day when they returned, the chip had disintegrated."

"Disintegrated?" Matt asked. "What do you mean by that? You mean disappeared, rotted, or dried up?"

"No. It more or less dissolved, and took everything traceable with it. There was a print of the object left in the package it was in, but the print had no organic or metallic signature to diagnose. It was like what was left was a type of picture of where the chip had been. But unlike where a human hand leaves a fingerprint, or a body moved usually leaves a DNA trace, there was nothing left to test. The swabs picked up no trace of any- thing that could be examined from the picture."

"All that's left to examine is the picture the chip left. Maybe examining the geometric shapes and patterns of the object can tell us something, but I don't have much confidence that examining what is essentially a picture of an object can provide the information that the actual object would have provided."

"Well, anyway," Matt returned, "if anything develops, keep me posted." "I will," the doctor answered. "I had high hopes of what we would find out about that foreign matter."

"How does Six find these places?" Tangie asked, as they turned off a paved highway and started bouncing on a dusty, bumpy, dirt road.

"Probably a safer safe house," Matt answered. "Although I don't know if any safe house is completely safe."

"I see the house there in the distance," he said, after the couple had drove for several miles.

"Watch out for the ditch coming up," Tangie ordered, as they came to a big dip in the road.

"Good thing there has been no rain," Matt responded, as he slowed the car down. "We wouldn't be able to cross this dry river bed. It's pretty deep." A couple minutes later, the couple arrived at the second safe house.

Matt parked their car right behind Mr. Six's car. Mr. Six stood in the doorway and waited to greet them.

"Let me congratulate you two for a job well done," Mr. Six said, and he clapped his hands while the two exited the car and walked to the doorway.

"I'm sure the NSA has top jobs waiting for you."

"You took care of a lot of bad guys, and developed a mind control system in your spare time. There's a lot of people who are going to be happy, and your work is going for the good of mankind."

"Do you have the key?"

"Yes," Matt answered. And he handed Mr. Six the drive, as they entered the lobby.

"Where's all of your weapons?" Mr. Six asked them.

"They're packed in the car," Tangie answered. "We don't plan to use them any time soon."

"I hope not," Mr. Six answered.

"This is some safe house," Matt quipped to Mr. Six, as they sat down. "Out in the middle of nowhere."

"This safe house is much safer," Mr. Six chimed back. "The perimeter is wider. There's miles of desert. It can even detect incoming missiles. It was just recently built. It took only six weeks. The government can work fast when they want to."

"With a dry moat," Tangie chimed in.

"That ditch assures no one easily rolls up on you here," Mr. Six responded. "But you won't need this place now that Stenner and his crew have been taken care of."

"I'm glad we don't need to stay here long," Tangie said. "It could be very boring staying out here for any extended period of time."

"It has a lot." Mr. Six responded. "It is a new facility, with all of the latest technology. It doesn't have an escape tunnel yet, but may not need one now."

"Here comes Mr. Dial."

Mr. Dial drove up and parked his pickup truck behind Matt and Tangie's vehicle. Mr. Six walked to the door and opened it.

"I see why you told me to drive my four-wheel drive truck," Mr. Dial said to Mr. Six. "That river bed is pretty deep."

"Yes," Mr. Six responded. "But it's not wide or wet."

"It's so great to see you two again," Mr. Dial said to Matt and Tangie, as he walked over and shook their hands.

"Those in the know extend their sincerest appreciation for a job well done. The president also sends his regards."

"Too bad there can be no record of what you did. No awards ceremonies. No public acknowledgement of any of what you have done. All we can do is ask you to forget everything so far, and we'll move forward."

"That's perfectly okay with us," Matt said.

"Yes," Tangie agreed. "All we want to think about is our careers from this day forward."

"And I look forward to seeing you in your new careers," Mr. Dial answered. "After you take off a couple weeks for some well-needed rest, the agency will be contacting you."

"And I believe you have delivered to Mr. Six something for me?" "Yes, they have," Mr. Six answered. He pulled the key out of his pocket

and handed it to Mr. Dial.

"Okay," Mr. Dial responded, as he pulled a cell phone looking device out of his pocket. "Let's authenticate the information, and make sure all of the encryption is removed."

Mr. Dial plugged the key into his device. The device had a screen that lit up. Mr. Dial scrolled through the information that appeared on the screen. He saw Matt and Tangie on the screen narrating the program. "Looks good!" Mr. Dial said as he scrolled down the information on

the screen. Each section of information had "Top Secret" at the top of the virtual document.

"Looks real good!" He turned off the device.

"Great work!" Mr. Dial said to Matt and Tangie. "This is the most top-secret document in the world."

"The CIA wants to control America. And they would have wielded a much more powerful hand with this information. But we have the upper hand on them now."

"At the proper time, you will be recognized for your groundbreaking accomplishment."

"Is everything on the key?" Mr. Six asked Mr. Dial. "Everything's there," Mr. Dial answered.

"Good!" Mr. Six responded.

He pulled out a pistol and shot Mr. Dial right between the eyes. Mr. Dial fell to the floor. Mr. Six pointed his gun at Matt and Tangie. They jumped back and raised their hands in the air. Mr. Six reached down and picked up the drive from the floor, while he kept his gun pointed at the couple.

"I suppose this is the time I give you brainiacs my complete story," Mr. Six said to them while he put the drive into his pocket with his free hand.

"I'll be happy to tell you about me, before I kill you."

"It all began when your God cast down a third of his angels from his heavenly home. We didn't want to play his game anymore, just like many humans on Earth."

"So, you're the devil?" Matt asked. "Indeed!" Mr. Six answered.

"I felt in my spirit there was something strange about you," Tangie said. "We have literally danced with the devil."

"Not strange to us," Mr. Six responded.

"Anyway, that was six million years ago," Mr. Six continued.

"Then your God decided to make human companions in his own image. We had a six-million-year head start over you humans to develop our civilization. That's why our technology is so far ahead of yours. Your technology is so primitive in our eyes."

"Technology?' Tangie asked. "You mean alien technology? So that's where aliens come from?"

"Correct." Mr. Six answered. "Ephesians Chapter Six, verse Twelve, 'For our struggle is not against flesh and blood, but against the rulers, against the authorities, against the powers of this dark world and against the spiritual forces of evil in the heavenly realms.'"

"But you're human," Matt said.

"We can take human form," Mr. Six responded. "In fact, we're integrating more and more into humans. That's why we abduct and integrate our genes into yours to produce human aliens."

"Your God didn't provide us the ability to reproduce. Many of us die in your atmosphere and environment. We will carry on as we colonize Earth by having your females reproduce aliens."

"The only problem is that the alien species are working against each other in many ways."

"After we were cast to Earth, we started having problems with each other. Over time we separated and developed into six alien species with six different looks, and six different rates of development. We became what you call the Moloch, Chemosh, Dagon, Belial, Beelzebub, and Satan. Some groups went off to other worlds on exoplanets but are coming back to reproduce. Each group wants its species to dominate."

"Aliens abduct other aliens. Each type wants to learn from each other, and become the dominant species. You could say there's a race between ETs for the human race."

"Which of the groups do you belong?" Matt asked. "Satan," Mr. Six answered.

"And your real name is not Six," Tangie surmised. "It is Lucifer." "Brilliant deduction," Mr. Six said to Tangie.

"So," Tangie said, "six million years on Earth and the cosmos, six different alien species. Lucifer takes the name Mr. Six. Six, six, six."

"Excellent," Mr. Six said. Your Christian Bible is the greatest book ever written, I have to admit. That's why we work so hard to defeat and diffuse it."

"So why do you abduct and mutilate animals?" Matt asked.

"We use their blood," Lucifer answered. We can't get enough human blood for translating to human form. And we study their genes to integrate their best characteristics into alien humans. For instance, animals can endure more heat and cold than humans."

"When we do become human, we take on all human characteristics. We get hungry and have to eat. We get thirsty and have to drink. We have emotions. We can be physically hurt and killed, just like Jesus when he took on human form. That's why I'll go to another form soon. We can shift to other forms."

"You can also change your voice to anybody's voice that you have heard," Matt said. "That's why you could imitate those agents' voices."

"That's easy as pie," Lucifer reiterated. "That's one of the terms you humans like to use."

"Your human culture changes every ten years or so. You are such interesting specimens to observe and study, especially Americans because you are never satisfied, and are always looking for the next best of everything." "You humans do almost as much damage to each other as we do. You

are so good at stealing, killing, and destroying each other that we learn things from you."

"But we never learned mind control. Thanks to you two brilliant minds, I now have that power at my disposal. There is no greater weapon than being able to telepathically make people do what you want them to do."

"The only thing I was really interested in getting from Level Four of the facility was that forever battery that's in your vehicle. Everything else they're working on in there was unstable and unnecessary for me to do my job."

"One of my workers was able to get a position on the team in Level Four. But he knew he couldn't smuggle that part out because the workers on Level Four are searched and scanned before they leave work. That's why he befriended Flo, believing she would innocently get it out. I was hoping it would make it to market and bring down those greedy oil companies." "Now you brought it right to me. I will have it to use to get around as long as I'm in human form, and not have to help make those monopolizing

oil companies and their political cronies richer."

"Some of the alien types were working with your people in the GOD facility. I know it was the Dagon demon aliens who didn't have a presence in your facility."

"They are probably the ones who abducted us," Matt surmised. "They probably put that chip in me to find out what was going on in there."

"Every alien type knew about the GOD facility, but not all of them were allowed to work in there."

"Abductions will only increase," Lucifer said. "Especially in America.

With mind control, my alien type will control the others."

"So, you knew much more about the facility than you originally told us, even the exits?" Tangie asked.

"I couldn't tell you everything," Lucifer answered. "That could have compromised my mission. Plus, you weren't supposed to know about the emergency exit unless you needed it. Flo didn't even know."

"One other thing," Matt spoke up, "and I don't expect you to answer, but I'm going to ask anyway."

"The DEA operation to apprehend the drugs, weapons, and the Columbian and Mexican smugglers on the Mexican coast that failed, and resulted in eleven dead DEA agents and a news reporter. It failed be- cause the smugglers knew the DEA was coming. You wouldn't have had something to do with the smugglers knowing that the DEA was coming, would you?"

"I refuse to answer that question," Mr. Six answered. So, you're right. I won't answer that question. You'll have to take that question to your grave." "I will say those jack-booted agents have a flair for the dramatics.

Unlike the CIA, the DEA likes publicity. They brought about their own demise."

"They were just doing their jobs," Tangie spoke up. "They were trying to make America and the world safer. Those people didn't deserve to be killed doing their jobs."

"Maybe they should do their job by not trying to invade other countries," Lucifer responded. "Maybe they have been watching too many John Wayne, Clint Eastwood, and Chuck Norris movies."

"I love American television. I'm sure you know of the American who is given credit for inventing television in nineteen twenty seven, Philo Taylor Farnsworth. The television was actually derived from alien technology."

"The history books say Farnsworth lived in a house without electricity when he was young. He didn't need electricity because he had an alien source of power. The Earth generates all kinds of energy for us to use. You humans still using fossil fuels for power is about the stupidest thing you do."

"But enough of this small talk."

Mr. Six backed up to the wall to a timer, as he held his gun pointed at the couple. He set the timer at ten minutes.

"There's enough explosives in this house to level a small town. This house is one big bomb. You know I'm good with bombs. Bomb making is my specialty. When this place blows, there won't be a trace of your bodies for anyone to identify."

"It's been nice working with you two. But I've got much more work to do. You know the devil never stops working. Throw me your car keys please."

Matt pulled his keys out of his pocket and did as commanded.

"You are two walking super brains, capable of accomplishing things the regular human brain has not learned to do, and hopefully will never learn to do. I will be the only one alive to possess that kind of knowledge and power."

"You two may go to heaven when I kill you, but you have made it possible for me to take a lot more people with me to hell. I'm gonna love turning believing Christians into non-believing sinners."

"Now, who do I shoot first? I better make up my mind fast. I've got less than seven minutes to take care of you and get a safe distance from here. Think I'll let Tangie see Matt die before I send her to heaven to be with your disgusting God."

Mr. Six pointed his gun at Matt's head. His finger started to squeeze the trigger. Matt turned his head and starred Mr. Six right in his eyes. Mr. Six looked stunned at the way Matt looked at him.

Then Tangie raised her head and looked into Mr. Six's eyes. He pointed his gun at her. He looked at her eyes and didn't like the way she looked at him. His finger eased up on the trigger. He turned his eyes back to Matt, then shifted back to Tangie. He wanted to look away from them but couldn't stop looking at their eyes, and couldn't stop them from starring at him.

His hand slowly turned the gun away from them. He had fear in his eyes as he looked down and saw his hand turning the gun toward himself.

He looked back up at Tangie and Matt. They were still staring in- tensely at him. He looked back at the gun, which was approaching his face. His body was frozen, as he looked back at the couple's eyes on him.

He opened his mouth, although he tried not to. He looked back at the couple still staring him down.

He put the gun barrel in his mouth. He pulled the trigger, and splattered his brains all over the wall behind him.

They watched him fall to the floor and drop the keys to their car. "Let's run!" Matt yelled, as he saw the timer was down to thirty seconds. Tangie picked up their car keys from the floor.

They ran out of the house, and paused at their vehicle.

"We don't have time to get it out from between the other two cars!" Matt called. "Let's just keep running!"

They ran down the dirt road, away from the house. "Times almost up!" Matt yelled, as they ran.

"We need to make it to that ditch!" Tangie yelled back. The timer went to zero. They leaped into the ditch.

The house blew up like a nuclear explosion. A mushroom cloud rose into the sky. The blast consumed the three vehicles that sat outside.

The fire shot out in all directions. The flames flew over Matt and Tangie, as they rolled to the bottom of the ditch. The ground shook.

Loose dirt ran down on the couple. They looked up and saw the flames flying over them at the top of the ditch.

After a few minutes, the flames subsided. They brushed the loose dirt off themselves and slowly climbed out of the ditch.

They stood at the top of the ditch and looked back at the burning pieces of what remained of the house, and the remains of the three vehicles which had burned to a crisp.

They looked around and saw smoldering tumbleweeds and sagebrush.

They looked down at the scorched ground.

Tangie looked at Matt.

"How did you do that?" she asked, while they brushed the dust off themselves.

"How did I do what?"

"How did you telepathically take over Lucifer's brain, command his occipital lobe to keep his eyes focused on us, while suppressing his frontal lobe's ability to reason, and make his cerebellum coordinate a physical action that his temporal lobe did not want to perform? That's true mind control! You did it!"

"What do you mean I did it?" he asked. "I thought YOU did it!" "Whatever happened," Tangie responded, "I've had enough of this

brain work."

"Me too."

"So, what do we do now?" she asked.

"Well," he answered, "I believe we can find grace and peace in Paradise Hills, New Mexico."

"And a little boy who needs some tender loving care," she added. "Yes, he does," Matt agreed.

They started walking down the dirt road, away from the smoke and dying flames.

"Do you think we're any good at hitchhiking?" Tangie asked.

"We better be, otherwise it's a long walk to Albuquerque. It's a long enough walk just to get back to a paved road where we can hitchhike."

THREE WEEKS LATER

Flo finished her sermon in the chapel at her orphanage. The sanctuary was filled with her orphan residents. Also attending were couples looking to adopt orphans, and many of the donors who contribute to Flo's orphan- age. Tangie and Matt sat on the front row. Jamie sat between them.

"This concludes my sermon today," Flo said from the pulpit as she closed her Bible.

"I pray you all got something from my message on forgiving."

"We need to be able to forgive, just like God forgives. If you're not able to forgive, and keep holding on to those negative feelings, it's like you're swallowing the poison that you think is harming the other person."

"Now, before I give the benediction, I want to give an invitation to anyone who may not have accepted Jesus as their Lord and Savior. Accepting and turning your life over to Jesus is the only way to get to heaven."

"You can be smart. You can be a good person. You can be an American hero. But if you don't have Jesus, you will be eternally lost to hell."

"Would you rather live with Jesus forever or would you rather spend eternity with the devil?"

"You can accept Jesus now, and we will pray with you."

"Jesus will not make you come to Him. But if you accept Him, He will accept you. It doesn't matter if you've lied, cheated, stolen, killed, or any kind of sin. Jesus will accept you."

"If anyone wants to accept Jesus, please raise your hand."

Tangie looked over at Jamie. She smiled, and tears started to roll down her face when she saw Jamie raise his hand. She looked over to Jamie's right side where Matt sat. She smiled and wept again when she saw Matt also raise his hand.

THE END

Be on the lookout for the upcoming novels by James A. Johnson.

1. **BEST SELLER©** – Marion Paris was once a bestselling author. However, Marion has not written a best seller in over 15 years. He believes he has one in the works when a former FBI agent wants to meet with him and provide information about a KKK faction in Arkansas he infiltrated to find why a former FBI infiltrator was killed. But the former FBI agent dies in an automobile accident on his way to meet Marion. Marion has reason to believe the former agent was murdered.

At the same time, another man finds out that Marion is re- turning to his hometown to write this book about the former FBI informant. He contacts Marion to get him to write a book on his brother's experience in the Mafia. Those revelations, however, may implicate some "respectable" citizens. The 'brother' also stole $2 million from the mafia, and wants Marion to give it back to them. The man wants Marion to pronounce his brother dead in his book so the mob will stop looking for him.

In both cases, the people involved want to eliminate Marion.

Does Marion solve the crimes, or just try to save himself?

This is the first of the Best Seller series, with Marion Paris, the unintentional sleuth, who finds himself involved in solving crimes.

2. **CHECKERED PAST©** – Murder, Greed. Blackmail, Fraud, Twisted Romance. A good book with the old New Orleans backdrop before hurricane Katrina. Pam McShan is a beautiful and aspiring CPA moving up the ladder at her CPA firm. The firm is about to promote her to a partner in the firm because of her good work. The CEO of the firm assigns her to audit their biggest client, First Cajun Bank.

Pam finds fraud at the bank. Prominent banking executives lose their jobs. The New Orleans newspaper writes a story about the scheme, and prints the story in Pam's hometown newspaper. Pam's boss is murdered. Some characters from her past that she had left behind come back into her life, and Pam's world is suddenly turned upside down.

3. **OBSESSIVE BEHAVIOR©** – Addiction, Corruption, Murder, Romance. Mike Lassiter is a young doctor in Birmingham, Alabama. Mike is also a sex addict. He loves his job, but loves his free time even better. He works at the VA hospital because he wants more free hours than the time involved in private practice would allow. Mike has a special 'talents' when it comes to loving women. He devotes most of his spare time working on his talent. When law enforcement closes down his favorite hangout for picking up women, he begins to feel that Birmingham is too conservative for him.

Mike decides to move to California, where he believes he will find more freedom to explore his sexual obsession. However, one of Mike's sexual adventures with a prominent San Francisco socialite leads to her murder, and Mike is charged with the crime. He is convicted and goes to prison, where the judge sentences him to spend his first six months in a women's prison. As part of the judge's rehab and punishment process, he orders that Mike not be allowed to interact or eat with the women, just see women he cannot have.

However, Mike finds out that the prison has its own rules. When there is a murder in the prison, Mike is blamed for the crime. He must work to prove he is innocent of two murders, while also helping a woman he meets in prison prove she did not commit the murder for which she is convicted.

4. **UPTOWN GHETTO©** – Racism, Murder, Corruption, Fraud. Socioeconomic and political cultures collide when Rob Lowery, a wealthy college graduate from a rich area of north Cleveland, Ohio decides to go to work for his father in the investment and real estate business. Part of Rob's job is to oversee the company's donations to charitable organizations. One of those organizations is in a Cleveland ghetto. Against his father's wishes, Rob visits the center, and finds the records are not up to date. Rob wants to return and help the center get its books in order. Rob also meets a street rapper called 2Quik. Rob and 2Quick forge a relationship as 2Quik introduces Rob to the ways of the streets, while Rob educates the rapper on life and issues on the other side of the fence.

Rob ask 2Quik to help him out at the community center when he finds out 2Quik has a keen insight for numbers. 2Quick has some questions about how some of the numbers are adding up at the center. Before he can get answers, 2Quick is murdered. The locals believe Rob or his father is responsible for 2Quick's death. Rob's friends and relatives tell him to get out of the ghetto before he is the next one to be killed. Rob promises 2Quick's mother that he will find out the cause of 2Quik's death.

5. **LIVING THE JAI LIFE** – The sport of Jai Alai (Pronounced Hi/ Ah/ Li) was once a very popular sport in America at the turn of the 20th century. The sport waned due to corruption, and other sports becoming more popular for gambling. A group of entrepreneurs and politicians in Miami ban together to bring back the sport. They build a new combination basketball and Jai Alai arena in an effort to bring the Black and Hispanic communities closer together. They also bring Hosea Jorge, the best and most popular Jai Alai player in Europe, to Miami to help reintroduce and repopularize the sport in America.

Their efforts come to the attention of some powerful people in Las Vegas, who want to gain control of the movement.

Jalen Williams, a promising City League basketball player, makes friends with Hosea after they run into each other in the arena. They start hanging out together, and begin teaching each other their sport.

The Vegas syndicate approaches Hosea, and try to bribe, then threaten him to throw some Jai Alai matches. Hosea refuses to go along with their schemes, and is murdered. Jalen witnesses the murder from a dark and distant part of the gym section of the arena. No one knew he was there.

Jalen curiously gets involves in trying to solve the murder and uncovering the cover up when he realizes law enforcement has been paid off to ignore the crime. Jalen decides to get closer to investigate the schemes by becoming a Jai Alai player.

6. **AMERICAN UBERLEBEN** – "Überleben" is German for "survival". This is a historic novel set in 1940's World War II. American paratroopers are assigned to jump behind enemy lines in eastern France to destroy an underground German command center in western Germany. Two black soldiers are assigned by the President to the unit. After the soldiers set up their camp, the racist commander sends the two black men out on a reconnaissance spy mission to scout the German targets and positions, hoping they will be captured or killed. After they leave, the Germans discover the camp.

When the two paratroopers return, they find the camp destroyed, and all of their fellow soldiers killed. The two men must decide whether to try to carry out the mission and return home, or just try to find a way to get back home.

7. **STALKING, MAINE** – The city of Stalking, Maine is a thriving port city. Lobster and Halibut fishing is their main industry, which makes the town prosperous and happy. The Russian Mob becomes interested in controlling and siphoning off the wealth of the fishing industry there. They send some people to the town to take over and monopolize the lobster trade, and also use prostitutes to bribe the local officials, and to keep them silent.

At the same time, a serial killer migrates to the city to get away from law enforcement who was closing in on him in Atlanta. He had killed several prostitutes.

A white female social worker of the all-white town goes to Chicago on a training seminar. She meets a black war veteran at the seminar. He works at a rehabilitation center, and suffers from Post Traumatic Stress Disorder (PTSD). She falls for him, and he falls for her. She asks him to relocate to her town. He is reluctant to become the first black resident of Stalking, but agrees to her wish. The town tries to cope, deal with, and resolve rising criminal activities, while trying to adjust and reclaim its peaceful and prosperous lifestyle.

8. **BEST SELLER 2** Corruption, Murder. Marion Paris is at it again. The New York City author from East St Louis, Missouri, prepares to write another book. He becomes an unintentional sleuth again, as he discovers criminal activity and murder within the company and people he plans to write about. His life is in danger once again.

9. **SOUTHERN DISCOMFORT** - Corruption, Murder, Cover-ups. Randy and his wife Donna love going to Monday night bible study at the county jail in Mishap, Alabama. Mishap is a city of about 10,000 people sitting on the Alabama-Florida line.

Randy and Donna believe their calling is to lead the incarcerated to the Lord, and help change their lives. Randy develops a special bond with a prisoner named Cornelius, who everyone calls Corn. Corn claims he did not kill his girlfriend, for which he is incarcerated. He tries to get Randy to help him prove his innocence by trying to get Randy to take notes and messages to people on the outside, which is against prison rules.

The town's life routine is disrupted when a tornado rips through Mishap, destroying the town, including the jail. Several inmates escape the destroyed facility. Law enforcement, including the FBI, try to capture the escapees. Most of the prisoners are found within three days. But law enforcement cannot find Corn. Corn goes on the run, as an expanded manhunt begins. He contacts Randy, and tries to get Randy to help him prove his innocence, and expose the corruption of law enforcement that put him behind bars.

10. **N...TIME -** What does the N stand for? Does it mean the end of time? Does it mean just in time? Is it the N word? Or another n word? Could it be...Nuclear? Take time to check out this psychological thriller.

Printed in the USA
CPSIA information can be obtained
at www.ICGtesting.com
LVHW021600030724
784600LV00008B/130